Lilian Jackson Braun composed her first poem at the age of two. She began writing her *Cat Who...* mysteries when one of her own Siamese cats mysteriously fell to its death from her apartment block. Since then, seventeen *Cat Who...* novels have been published, all featuring the very talented Koko and Yum Yum, Siamese cats with a bent for detection. She is currently working on the next novel in this internationally bestselling series. There are now over three million *Cat Who...* mysteries in print around the world.

Lilian Jackson Braun and her husband, Earl, live with their two Siamese cats, Koko III and Pitti Sing, in the mountains of North Carolina.

*Also by Lilian Jackson Braun*

The Cat Who Ate Danish Modern
The Cat Who Turned On and Off
The Cat Who Saw Red
The Cat Who Played Brahms
The Cat Who Played Post Office
The Cat Who Knew Shakespeare
The Cat Who Sniffed Glue
The Cat Who Went Underground
The Cat Who Talked To Ghosts
The Cat Who Lived High
The Cat Who Knew a Cardinal
The Cat Who Moved a Mountain
The Cat Who Wasn't There
The Cat Who Went Into the Closet
The Cat Who Came to Breakfast
The Cat Who Blew the Whistle

# The Cat Who Could Read Backwards

## Lilian Jackson Braun

HEADLINE

First published in Great Britain in 1995
by HEADLINE BOOK PUBLISHING

10 9 8 7 6 5 4 3 2 1

ISBN 0 7472 5034 0

Printed and bound in Great Britain by
Cox & Wyman Ltd, Reading, Berks

HEADLINE BOOK PUBLISHING
A division of Hodder Headline PLC
338 Euston Road
London NW1 3BH

# The Cat Who Could Read Backwards

# CHAPTER ONE

Jim Qwilleran, whose name had confounded typesetters and proofreaders for two decades, arrived fifteen minutes early for his appointment with the managing editor of the *Daily Fluxion*.

In the reception room he picked up a copy of the early edition and studied the front page. He read the weather prediction (unseasonably warm) and the circulation figures (427,463) and the publisher's slogan snobbishly printed in Latin (*Fiat Flux*).

He read the lead story on a murder trial and the secondary lead on the gubernatorial race, in which he found two typographical errors. He noticed that the art museum had failed to get its million-dollar grant, but he skipped the details. He bypassed another feature about a kitten trapped in a drainpipe, but he read everything else: *Cop Nabs Hood in Gun Tiff. Probe Stripper Feud in Loop. Stocks Soar as Tax Talk Irks Dems.*

Qwilleran could hear familiar noises beyond a glass-paneled door—typewriters clattering, teletypes jigging, telephones screaming. At the sound his ample pepper-and-salt moustache bristled, and he smoothed it with his knuckles. Aching for a sight of the bustle and clutter that constituted the City Room before a deadline, he walked to the door for a squint through the glass.

The sounds were authentic, but the scene—he discovered—was all wrong. The Venetian blinds were straight. The desks were tidy and unscarred. Crumpled copy paper and slashed newspapers that should have been on the floor were collected in wire wastebaskets. As he contemplated the scene with dismay, an alien sound reached his ears—one that did not harmonize with the background music of any city rooms he had known. Then he noticed a copyboy feeding yellow pencils into a small moaning contraption. Qwilleran stared at the thing. An electric pencil sharpener! He had never thought it would come to this. It reminded him how long he had been out of touch.

Another copyboy in tennis shoes bounced out of the City Room and said, "Mr. Qwilleran? You can come in now."

Qwilleran followed him to the cubicle where a young managing editor was waiting with a sincere handshake and a sincere smile. "So you're Jim Qwilleran! I've heard a lot about you."

Qwilleran wondered how much—and how bad. In the job résumé he had mailed to the *Daily Fluxion* his career traced a dubious curve: sports writer, police reporter, war correspondent, winner of the Publishers' Trophy, author of a book on urban crime. Then came a succession of short-term jobs on smaller and smaller newspapers, followed by a long period of unemployment—or no jobs worth listing.

The managing editor said, "I remember your coverage of the trial that won you the Publishers' Trophy. I was a cub reporter at the time and a great admirer of yours."

By the man's age and schooled manner, Qwilleran recognized him as the new breed of editor—one of the precision-honed generation who approached newspapering as a science rather than a holy cause. Qwilleran had always worked for the other kind—the old-fashioned nail-spitting crusaders.

The editor was saying, "With your background you may be disappointed in our offer. All we have for you is a desk in the Feature Department, but we'd like you to take it until something turns up cityside."

"And until I've proved I can stay on the job?" Qwilleran said, looking the man in the eye. He had been through a humbling experience; now the problem was to strike the right chord of humility and confidence.

"That goes without saying. How are you getting along?"

"So far, so good. The important thing is to get back on a newspaper. I wore out my welcome in several cities before I got smart. That's why I wanted to come here. Strange town—lively paper—new challenge. I think I can make it work."

"Sure you can!" said the editor, squaring his jaw. "And here's what we have in mind for you. We need an art writer."

"An art writer!" Qwilleran winced and mentally composed a headline: *Vet Newsman Put to Pasture.*

"Know anything about art?"

Qwilleran was honest. He said, "I don't know the Venus de Milo from the Statue of Liberty."

"You're exactly what we want! The less you know, the fresher your viewpoint. Art is booming in this town, and we need to give it more coverage. Our art critic writes a column twice a week, but we want an experienced newsman to scout stories about the artists themselves. There's plenty of material. These days, as you probably know, artists are more plentiful than cats and dogs."

Qwilleran combed his moustache with his knuckles.

The editor continued in a positive vein. "You'll report to the feature editor, but you can dig up your own assignments. We'll want you to get around on the beat, meet a lot of artists, shake a few hands, make friends for the paper."

Qwilleran silently composed another headline: *Journalist Sinks to Role of Glad-hander*. But he needed the job. Necessity battled with conscience. "Well," he said, "I don't know—"

"It will be a nice clean beat, and you'll meet some decent people for a change. You've probably had your fill of mobsters and con men."

Qwilleran's twitching moustache was trying to say who-the-hell-wants-a-nice-clean-beat, but its owner maintained a diplomatic silence.

The editor consulted his watch and stood up. "Why don't you go upstairs and talk it over with Arch Riker? He can—"

"Arch Riker! What's he doing here?"

"He's feature editor. Know him?"

"We worked together in Chicago—years ago."

"Good! He'll give you all the details. And I hope you decide to join the *Flux*." The editor extended his hand and smiled a measured smile.

Qwilleran wandered out through the City Room again—past the rows of white shirts with sleeves at three-quarter mast, past the heads bent obliviously over typewriters, past the inevitable girl reporter. She was the only one who gave him an inquisitive look, and he stretched to his full six-feet-two, reined in the superfluous ten pounds that pushed at his belt buckle, and passed a preening hand over his head. Like his upper lip, it still boasted three black hairs for every one that was gray.

Upstairs he found Arch Riker presiding over a roomful of desks, typewriters and telephones—all in a single shade of pea green.

"Pretty fancy, isn't it?" Arch said apologetically. "They call it Eye-Ease Olive. Everybody has to be pampered these days. Personally, I think it looks bilious."

The Feature Department was a small edition of the City

Room—without the smolder of urgency. Serenity filled the room like a mist. Everyone seemed to be ten years older than the crew in the City Room, and Arch himself was plumper and balder than he used to be.

"Jim, it's great to see you again," he said. "Do you still spell your name with that ridiculous W?"

"It's a respectable Scottish spelling," Qwilleran protested.

"And I see you haven't got rid of that overgrown moustache."

"It's my only war souvenir." The knuckles smoothed it affectionately.

"How's your wife, Jim?"

"You mean my ex-wife?"

"Oh, I didn't know. Sorry."

"Let's skip that. . . . What's this job you've got for me?"

"It's a snap. You can do a Sunday piece for us if you want to start today."

"I haven't said I'll take the job yet."

"You'll take it," Arch said. "It's just right for you."

"Considering my recent reputation, you mean?"

"Are you going to be touchy? Forget it. Quit needling yourself."

Qwilleran parted his moustache thoughtfully. "I suppose I could give it a try. Want me to do a trial assignment?"

"Anything you say."

"Got any leads?"

"Yes." Arch Riker drew a pink sheet of paper from a tickler file. "How much did the boss tell you?"

"He didn't tell me anything," Qwilleran said, "except that he wants human-interest stuff on artists."

"Well, he sent up a pink memo suggesting a story on a guy called Cal Halapay."

"So?"

"Here at the *Flux* we have a color code. A blue memo

means *For Your Information*. Yellow means *Casual Suggestion*. But pink means *Jump, Man, Jump*."

"What's so urgent about Cal Halapay?"

"Under the circumstances it might be better if you didn't know the background. Just go out there cold, meet this Halapay person, and write something readable. You know all the tricks."

"Where do I find him?"

"Call his office, I suppose. He's a commercial artist and head of a successful agency, but he does oil paintings in his spare time. He paints pictures of kids. They're very popular. Kids with curly hair and rosy cheeks. They look apoplectic, but people seem to buy them. . . . Say, do you want lunch? We could go to the Press Club."

Qwilleran's moustache sprang to attention. Once upon a time press clubs had been his life, his love, his hobby, his home, his inspiration.

This one was across the street from the new police headquarters, in a sooty limestone fortress with barred windows that had once been the county jail. The stone steps, bowl-shaped with age, held the evidence of an unseasonable February thaw. In the lobby the ancient woodwork gleamed red under countless coats of varnish.

"We can eat in the bar," Arch said, "or we can go upstairs to the dining room. They've got tablecloths up there."

"Let's eat down here," Qwilleran said.

It was dim and noisy in the bar. Conversation was high-key, with confidential undertones. Qwilleran knew it well. It meant that rumors were circulating, campaigns were being launched, and cases were getting solved unofficially over a beer and a hamburger.

They found two empty stools at the bar and were confronted by a bartender wearing a red vest and a conspiratorial smile that brimmed with inside information. Qwilleran recalled that some of his best story tips had come from Press Club bartenders.

"Scotch and water," Arch ordered.

Qwilleran said, "Double tomato juice on the rocks."

"Tom-tom on the rocks," said the bartender. "You want a squeeze of lime and a shot of Worcestershire?"

"No, thanks."

"That's the way I fix it for my friend the mayor when he comes in here." There was more of the authoritative smile.

"No, thanks."

"How about a drop of Tabasco to give it a bite?"

"No, just pour it straight."

The bartender's mouth turned down at the corners, and Arch said to him, "This is Jim Qwilleran, a new staffer. He doesn't realize you're an artist. . . . Jim, this is Bruno. He gives his drinks a lot of personal expression."

Behind Qwilleran an earsplitting voice said, "I'll take less expression and a bigger shot of liquor. Hey, Bruno, make me a martini, and leave out the garbage. No olive, lemon twist, anchovy or pickled unborn tomato."

Qwilleran turned and faced a cigar clamped between grinning teeth, its size vastly out of proportion to the slender young man who smoked it. The black cord hanging from his breast pocket was obviously attached to a light meter. He was noisy. He was cocky. He was enjoying himself. Qwilleran liked him.

"This clown," Arch said to Qwilleran, "is Odd Bunsen from the Photo Lab. . . . Odd, this is Jim Qwilleran, old friend of mine. We hope he's joining the *Flux* staff."

The photographer extended a quick hand. "Jim, glad to meet you. Care for a cigar?"

"I use a pipe. Thanks just the same."

13

Odd studied Qwilleran's luxuriant moustache with interest. "That shrubbery's getting out of hand. Aren't you afraid of brush fires?"

Arch said to Qwilleran, "The black string hanging out of Mr. Bunsen's pocket is what we use to tie his head on. But he's a useful man. He has more information than the reference library. Maybe he can fill you in on Cal Halapay."

"Sure," said the photographer. "What do you want to know? He's got a sharp-looking wife, 34-22-32."

"Who is this Halapay, anyway?" Qwilleran asked.

Odd Bunsen consulted his cigar smoke briefly. "Commercial artist. Runs a big ad agency. Personally worth a few million. Lives in Lost Lake Hills. Beautiful house, big studio where he paints, two swimming pools. Two, did you get that? With water being so scarce, he probably fills one with bourbon."

"Any family?"

"Two or three kids. Gorgeous wife. Halapay owns an island in the Caribbean and a ranch in Oregon and a couple of private planes. Everything money can buy. And he's not tight with his dough. He's a good joe."

"What about these pictures he paints?"

"Sharp! Real sharp," said Odd. "I've got one hanging in my living room. After I photographed Halapay's wife at a charity ball last fall, he gave me a painting. Couple of kids with curly hair. . . . Well, I've got to go and eat now. There's a one o'clock assignment on the board."

Arch drained his drink and said to Qwilleran, "Talk to Halapay and size up the photo possibilities, and then we'll try to assign Odd Bunsen. He's our best man. Maybe he could try some color shots. It wouldn't hurt to do this layout in color."

"That pink memo has you straining a bit, hasn't it?" Qwilleran said. "What's the connection between Halapay and the *Daily Fluxion*?"

"I'm having another drink," Arch said. "Want another tomato juice?"

Qwilleran let the question drop, but he said, "Just give me one straight answer, Arch. Why are they offering me this art beat? Me, of all people."

"Because that's the way newspapers do things. They assign baseball experts as drama critics and church news writers to the nightclub beat. You know that as well as I do."

Qwilleran nodded and stroked his moustache sadly. Then he said, "What about this art critic you have on the staff? If I take the job, do I work with him? Or her, as the case may be?"

"It's a guy," Arch told him. "He writes critical reviews, and you'll be doing straight reporting and personality stories. I don't think there'll be any conflict."

"Does he work in our department?"

"No, he never comes to the office. He does his column at home, puts it on tape and sends it down by messenger once or twice a week. We have to transcribe it. It's a fat nuisance."

"What keeps him away? Doesn't he like pea green?"

"Don't ask me. That's his arrangement with the front office. He has a neat contract with the *Flux.*"

"What's the fellow like?"

"Aloof. Opinionated. Hard to get along with."

"That's nice. Is he young or old?"

"In between. He lives alone—with a cat, if you can picture that! A lot of people think the cat writes the column, and they may be right."

"Is his stuff any good?"

"*He* thinks so. And the brass evidently thinks so." Arch shifted around on the barstool while he weighed his next remark. "There's a rumor that the *Flux* has the guy heavily insured."

"What's so valuable about an art critic?"

"This one's got that certain magic that newspapers love; he's controversial! His column pulls hundreds of letters a week. No, thousands!"

"What kind of letters?"

"Angry ones. Sugary ones. Hysterical ones. The arty readers hate his guts; the others think he's the greatest, and they get to brawling among themselves. He manages to keep the whole city stirred up. Do you know what our last survey showed? The art page has a bigger readership than the sports section! Now you know and I know that's an unnatural situation."

"You must have a lot of art buffs in this town," Qwilleran said.

"You don't have to like art to enjoy our art column; you just have to like blood."

"But what do they fight about?"

"You'll find out."

"I can understand controversy in sports and politics, but art is art, isn't it?"

"That's what I used to think," said Arch. "When I took over the feature desk, I had this simpleminded notion that art was something precious—for beautiful people who had beautiful thoughts. Man, did I lose that dream in a hurry! Art has gone democratic. In this town it's the greatest fad since canasta, and anybody can play. People buy paintings instead of swimming pools."

Qwilleran chewed the ice in his tomato juice and pondered the mysteries of this beat the *Daily Fluxion* was offering him. "By the way," he said, "what's the critic's name?"

"George Bonifield Mountclemens."

"Say that again, please?"

"George Bonifield Mountclemens—the Third!"

"That's a stickful! Does he use all three names like that?"

"All three names, all nine syllables, all twenty-eight letters

16

plus the numerals! Twice a week we try to fit his by-line into a standard column width. It can't be done, except sideways. And he doesn't permit any abbreviations, hyphens, contractions or amputations!"

Qwilleran gave Arch a close look. "You don't like him much, do you?"

Arch shrugged. "I can take him or leave him. Actually I never see the guy. I just see the artists who come to the office wanting to punch him in the teeth."

"George Bonifield Mountclemens III!" Qwilleran shook his head in amazement.

"Even his name infuriates some of our readers," Arch said. "They want to know who does he think he is."

"Keep talking. I'm beginning to like this job. The boss said it was a nice wholesome beat, and I was afraid I'd be working with a bunch of saints."

"Don't let him kid you. All the artists in this town hate each other, and all the art-lovers take sides. Then everybody plays rough. It's like football only dirtier. Name-calling, back-biting, double-crossing—" Arch slid off his barstool. "Come on, let's get a corned beef sandwich."

The blood of several old war-horses that flowed through Qwilleran's veins began to churn a little faster. His moustache almost smiled. "Okay, I'll take it," he said. "I'll take the job."

# CHAPTER TWO

It was Qwilleran's first day on the job at the *Daily Fluxion*. He moved into one of the pea green desks in the Feature Department and got himself a supply of yellow pencils. He noticed that the pea green telephone was stenciled with an official reminder: *Be Nice to People*. He tried the pea green typewriter by poking out, "The time of many murders is after midnight." Then he telephoned the *Fluxion* garage to request a staff car for the trip to Lost Lake Hills.

To reach the fashionable exurb fifteen miles beyond the city limits, Qwilleran drove through complacent suburbs and past winter-brown farms patched with snow. He had plenty of time to think about this interview with Cal Halapay, and he wondered if the Qwilleran Method would still work. In the old days he had been famous for a brotherly approach that put interviewees at ease. It was composed of two parts sympathy, two parts professional curiosity, and one part low blood pressure, and it had won confidences from old ladies, juvenile delinquents, pretty girls, college presidents and crooks.

Nevertheless, he felt qualms about the Halapay assignment. It had been a long time since he had done an interview, and artists were not his specialty. He suspected they spoke a secret language. On the other hand, Halapay was an advertising executive, and he might hand over a mimeographed release prepared by his public-relations office. Qwilleran's moustache shuddered.

It had always been the newsman's habit to compose the opening paragraph of his story in advance. It never worked, but he did it as a limbering-up exercise. Now—on the road to Lost Lake Hills—he made a few starts at the Halapay story.

He thought he might say, "When Cal Halapay leaves his plush executive suite at the end of the day, he forgets the cutthroat competition of the advertising rat race and finds relaxation in—" No, that was trite.

He tried again. "A multimillionaire advertising man with a beautiful wife (34-22-32) and two swimming pools (one filled with champagne, according to legend) admits he lives a double life. In painting poignant portraits of children, he escapes—" No, that was sensationalism.

Qwilleran recalled his brief employment with a newsmagazine and made another attempt in the crunchy style favored by that publication. "With an ascot folded in the throatline of his custom-made Italian silk sports shirt, the handsome, graying, six-foot-two czar of an advertising empire spends his spare time—"

Qwilleran guessed that a man of Halapay's accomplishments must be that tall, that gray, and that impressive. He would probably have a winter tan as well.

"With a blue foulard ascot accentuating his Caribbean tan—"

Lost Lake Road ended abruptly at a massive iron gate set in a fieldstone wall that looked impregnable and expensive. Qwilleran braked the car and glanced around for signs of a caretaker.

Almost immediately a recorded voice coming from the

gatepost said pleasantly, "Please face the pylon at your left and announce your name clearly."

He rolled down the car window and said, "Qwilleran from the *Daily Fluxion*."

"Thank you," murmured the gatepost.

The gate swung open, and the newsman drove into the estate, following a road that meandered through a tall stand of pines. It ended in a severely landscaped winter garden—all pebbles, boulders and evergreens, with arched bridges crossing small frozen ponds. In this setting, bleak but picturesque, stood a rambling house. It was contemporary in style with gently curving rooflines and opaque glass walls that looked like rice paper. Qwilleran revised his opening line about the Italian sports shirt. Halapay probably knocked around his million-dollar pagoda in a silk kimono.

At the entrance door, which appeared to be carved out of ivory, Qwilleran found something that resembled a doorbell and reached toward it, but before his finger touched the button, the surrounding panel glowed with a blue-green light and chimes could be heard indoors. These were followed by the bark of a dog, or two or three. There was a sharp command, a moment of silent obedience, and a briskly opened door.

"Good morning. I'm Qwilleran from the *Daily Fluxion*," the newsman said to a curly-haired, pink-faced youth in sweat shirt and dungarees, and before he could add, "Is your father home?" the young man said amiably, "Come in, sir. Here's your passport." He handed over a fuzzy snapshot of a heavily moustached face peering anxiously from the window of a car.

"That's me!" said Qwilleran in astonishment.

"Taken at the gate before you drove in," the young man said with obvious delight. "It's spooky, isn't it? Here, let me take your topcoat. I hope you don't mind the dogs. They're sort of friendly. They love visitors. This one is the mother.

She's four years old. The pups are from her last litter. Do you like blue terriers?"

Qwilleran said, "I—"

"Everyone wants Yorkshires these days, but I like the Kerry Blues. They've got beautiful coats, haven't they? Did you have any trouble finding the place? We have a cat, too, but she's pregnant, and she sleeps all the time. I think it's going to snow. I hope so. The skiing has been lousy this year—"

Qwilleran, who prided himself on conducting interviews without making notes, was taking mental inventory of the house: white marble foyer with fish pool and tropical tree probably fourteen feet high. Skylight two stories overhead. Sunken living room carpeted with something like white raccoon. Fireplace in a shiny black wall. Probably onyx. He noticed also that the boy had a hole in his sleeve and was padding around in sweat socks. The flow of chatter had not ceased.

"Would you like to sit in the living room, Mr. Qwilleran? Or do you want to go right to the studio? It's more comfortable in the studio, if you don't mind the smell. Some people are allergic to turpentine. Would you like a Coke or something? Allergies are funny things. I'm allergic to crustaceans. That burns me up, because I'm crazy about lobster—"

Qwilleran was waiting for a chance to say, "Is your father home?" when the young man said, "My secretary tells me you want to do a story on my paintings. Let's go into my studio. Do you want to ask questions, or shall I just talk?"

Qwilleran gulped and said, "Frankly, I was expecting you to be a much older—"

"I'm a boy wonder," said Halapay without smiling. "I made my first million before I was twenty-one. I'm twenty-nine now. I seem to have a genius for making money. Do you believe in genius? It's spooky, really. Here's a picture of me when I was married. My wife looks Oriental, doesn't she?

21

She's out taking an art lesson this morning, but you'll meet her after lunch. We designed the house to go with her looks. Would you like some coffee? I'll stir up the housekeeper if you want coffee. Let's face it, I look boyish and I always will. There's a bar in the studio if you'd rather have a drink."

The studio had a painty aroma, a good deal of clutter, and one vast wall of glass overlooking a white frozen lake. Halapay flicked a switch, and a filmy shade unfolded from the ceiling to screen out the glare. He touched another control, and doors glided open to reveal a bigger liquor supply than the Press Club had on its backbar.

Qwilleran said he preferred coffee, so Halapay pressed a button and gave the order to a brass grille mounted on the wall. He also handed Qwilleran an odd-shaped bottle from the bar.

"This is a liqueur I brought back from South America," he said. "You can't buy it here. Take it home with you. How do you like the view from this window? Sensational, isn't it? That's a man-made lake. The landscaping alone cost me half a million. Do you want a doughnut with your coffee? These are my paintings on the wall. Do you like them?"

The studio walls were covered with framed canvases—portraits of small boys and girls with curly hair and cheeks like red apples. Everywhere Qwilleran looked there were red apples.

"Pick out a painting," said Halapay, "and take it home with you—compliments of the artist. The large ones sell for five hundred dollars. Take a big one. Do you have any kids? We have two girls. That's their picture on the stereo cabinet. Cindy is eight and Susan is six."

Qwilleran studied the photograph of Halapay's daughters. Like their mother they had almond eyes and classically straight hair, and he said, "How come you paint nothing but children with curly hair and rosy cheeks?"

"You should go to the Valentine Ball on Saturday night. We're having a great jazz combo. Do you know about the ball? It's the annual Valentine party at the art club. We're all going in costume representing famous lovers. Would you like to go? You don't have to dress up, if masquerading doesn't appeal to you. It's twenty dollars a couple. Here, let me give you a pair of tickets."

"Getting back to your paintings," said Qwilleran, "I'm curious to know why you specialize in kids. Why not landscapes?"

"I think you should write up the ball in your column," Halapay said. "It's the biggest event of the year at the club. I'm chairman, and my wife's very photogenic. Do you like art? Everyone in the art field will be there."

"Including George Bonifield Mountclemens III, I suppose," said Qwilleran, in a tone intended to be jocular.

Without any change in his expressionless delivery, Halapay said. "That fraud! If that fraud showed his face in the outer lobby of the club, they'd throw him out. I hope he isn't a close friend of yours. I have no use for that character. He doesn't know anything about art, but he poses as an authority, and your paper lets him crucify established artists. They're letting him corrupt the entire art atmosphere of the city. They should get smart and unload him."

"I'm new on this beat," said Qwilleran, as Halapay stopped for breath, "and I'm no expert—"

"Just to prove what a fraud your critic is—he builds up Zoe Lambreth as a great artist. Did you ever see her stuff? It's a hoax. You go and see her paintings at the Lambreth Gallery, and you'll see what I mean. No reputable gallery would accept her work, so she had to marry an art dealer. There are tricks in all trades. As for her husband, he's nothing but a bookkeeper who got into the art racket, and I do mean racket. Here comes Tom with the coffee."

A houseboy dressed in soiled chinos and a half-buttoned shirt appeared with a tray, which he banged down on a table with a lack of grace. He gave Qwilleran an unfriendly stare.

Halapay said, "I wonder if we ought to have a sandwich with this. It's almost lunchtime. What do you want to know about my work? Go ahead and ask some questions. Don't you want to make notes?"

"I'd like to know," said Qwilleran, "why you specialize in painting children."

The artist lapsed into a thoughtful silence, his first since Qwilleran's arrival. Then he said, "Zoe Lambreth seems to have this big connection with Mountclemens. It would be interesting to know how she manages it. I could make a few guesses—not for publication. Why don't you dig into the situation? You might come up with a juicy exposé and get Mountclemens fired. Then you could be art critic."

"I don't want—" Qwilleran began.

"If your paper doesn't clean up that mess—and clean it up soon—they're going to start feeling it where it hurts. I wouldn't mind a hot dog with this coffee. Do you want a hot dog?"

At five-thirty that afternoon Qwilleran fled to the warm, varnished sanctuary of the Press Club, where he had agreed to meet Arch Riker. Arch wanted a quick drink on the way home. Qwilleran wanted an explanation.

He told Bruno curtly, "Tomato juice on the rocks. No lime, no Worcestershire, no Tabasco." To Arch he said, "Thanks, pal. Thanks for the welcome celebration."

"What do you mean?"

"Was that an initiation gag?"

"I don't know what you're talking about."

"I'm talking about that assignment to interview Cal Halapay. Was that a practical joke? You couldn't have been serious. The guy's a nut."

Arch said, "Well, you know how artists are. Individualists. What happened?"

"Nothing happened. Nothing I could possibly use in a story—and it took six hours to find it out. Halapay lives in this rambling house about the size of a junior high school, only it's sort of Japanese. And it's wired to do all kinds of tricks. The inside is wild. There's one wall made of glass rods hanging like icicles. They move when you walk past and sound like a xylophone that needs tuning."

"Well, why not? He's got to spend his dough somehow."

"I know, but wait till I finish. There's all this expensive stage setting, and then out comes Cal Halapay padding around in stocking feet and wearing a sweat shirt with a big hole in the elbow. And he looks about fifteen years old."

"Yes, I've heard he's youthful-looking—for a millionaire," Arch said.

"That's another thing. He keeps boasting about his money and trying to force presents on you. I had to fight off cigars, liquor, a $500 painting, a frozen turkey from his ranch in Oregon, and a Kerry Blue puppy. After lunch his wife showed up, and I was afraid his generosity would exceed the bounds of propriety. Incidentally, Mrs. Halapay is quite a dish."

"You're making me envious. What did you have for lunch? Ostrich tongues?"

"Hot dogs. Served by a houseboy with the charm of a gorilla."

"You got a free lunch. What are you griping about?"

"Halapay. He won't answer questions."

"He refuses?" Arch asked in surprise.

"He ignores them. You can't pin him down. He wanders from progressive jazz to primitive masks he collected in Peru to pregnant cats. I had more luck communicating with the gatepost than with that boy wonder."

"Did you get anything at all?"

"I saw his paintings, of course, and I found out about a blast the art club is giving on Saturday night. I think I might go."

"What did you think of his paintings?"

"They're slightly monotonous. All those red-apple cheeks! But I made a discovery. In all those pictures of kids, Cal Halapay is painting himself. I think he's enchanted with his own looks. Curly hair. Pink complexion."

Arch said, "I agree this isn't going to make the kind of story the boss wants. It sounds like *The Arabian Nights*."

"Do we have to run a story?"

"You saw the color of the memo. Pink!"

Qwilleran massaged his moustache. After a while he said, "The only time I got a direct answer to a question was when I mentioned George Bonifield Mountclemens."

Arch put down his drink. "What did Halapay say?"

"He exploded—in a controlled sort of way. Basically, he says Mountclemens isn't qualified to judge art."

"That figures. Halapay had a one-man show about a year ago, and our critic roasted him alive. The readers loved it. It cheered their black hearts to know that a successful money-man could be a failure at something. But it was a bitter blow to Halapay. He discovered his money could buy anything but a good art review."

"I weep for him. What about the other newspaper? Did they criticize his work, too?"

"They don't have a critic. Just a nice old lady reporter who covers the art openings and gushes about everything. They play it safe."

Qwilleran said, "So Halapay's a bad sport!"

"Yes, and you don't know how bad," said Arch, pulling his barstool closer to Qwilleran's. "Ever since that episode, he's been trying to bankrupt the *Flux*. He's withdrawn a lot of advertising linage and switched it over to the other paper. That hurts! Especially since he controls most of the food and fashion advertising in town. He's even trying to turn other admen against the *Flux*. It's serious."

Qwilleran grimaced in disbelief. "And I'm supposed to write a story buttering up that skunk, so the advertising department can get the linage back again?"

"Frankly, it would help. It would take the heat off."

"I don't like it."

"Don't go fastidious on me," Arch pleaded. "Just write a folksy piece about an interesting guy who wears old clothes around the house, takes his shoes off, keeps cats and dogs, eats wieners for lunch. You know how to do it."

"I don't like it."

"I'm not asking you to lie. Just be selective, that's all. Skip the part about the glass icicles and the half-million-dollar lake and the visits in South America, and bear down on the turkey farm and his lovely wife and the adorable kiddies."

Qwilleran brooded over it. "I suppose that's called practical newspapering."

"It helps pay the bills."

"I don't like it," said Qwilleran, "but if you're in that bad of a bind, I'll see what I can do." He raised his tomato juice glass. "Halapay or hell-to-pay!"

"Don't be cute. I've had a hard day."

"I'd like to read some of Mountclemens' reviews. Have you got them around?"

"On file in the library," Arch said.

"I want to see what he wrote about an artist named Zoe Lambreth. Halapay hinted at a shady connection between

Mrs. Lambreth and Mountclemens. Know anything about that?"

"I just process his copy. I don't peek under his window shades," said Arch, and he gave Qwilleran a good-night slap on the back.

# CHAPTER THREE

Qwilleran, wearing the newer and darker of his two suits, went alone to the Valentine Ball at the art club, which—he discovered—was called the Turp and Chisel. The club had originated forty years before in the back room of a blind pig. Now it occupied the top floor of the best hotel; its membership was large and fashionable; and the impecunious Bohemians who had founded the fraternity had become old, staid and full of dollars.

Upon his arrival at the ball, Qwilleran was able to wander unrecognized about the premises of the Turp and Chisel. He found a sumptuous lounge, a dining room, and a very busy bar. The games room, paneled with old barnwood, offered everything from darts to dominoes. In the ballroom, tables were draped with red and white cloths, and an orchestra played innocuous tunes.

He asked for the Halapay table and was greeted by Sandra Halapay wearing a white kimono of stiff embroidered silk. Exaggerated makeup made her almond eyes even more exotic.

"I was afraid you wouldn't come," she said, holding his hand long after the handshake had ended and delighting him with a rippling laugh.

"The invitation was irresistible, Mrs. Halapay," said Qwilleran. Then he surprised himself by bending over her hand and brushing it with his moustache.

"Please call me Sandy," she said. "Did you come alone? To a Lovers' Ball?"

"Yes. I represent Narcissus."

Sandy trilled with merriment. "You newspaper people are so clever!"

She was lyrically tall and lovely, Qwilleran decided, and tonight she was charmingly relaxed as wives often are when their husbands are absent.

"Cal is chairman of the ball," she said, "and he's flitting around, so you can be my date."

Her eyes were roguish as well as exotic.

Then Sandy, changing to a formal tone that rang hollow, introduced the others who were seated at the table. They were members of Cal's committee, she explained pointedly. A Mr. and Mrs. Riggs or Biggs were in French period costume. A short fleshy couple named Buchwalter, who seemed to be having a dull time, were garbed as peasants. There was also Mae Sisler, art reporter from the other newspaper.

Qwilleran gave her a fraternal bow, at the same time estimating that she was ten years past retirement age.

Mae Sisler gave him a bony hand and said in a thin voice, "Your Mr. Mountclemens is a very naughty boy, but you look like a nice young man."

"Thank you," said Qwilleran. "No one has called me a young man for twenty years."

"You'll like your new job," she predicted. "You'll meet lovely people."

Sandy leaned close to Qwilleran and said, "You look so romantic in that moustache. I wanted Cal to grow one so he would look halfway grown-up, but he resisted the suggestion.

He looks like such an infant. Don't you think so?" She laughed musically.

Qwilleran said, "It's true he appears youthful."

"I think he's retarded somehow. In another few years people will think he's my son. Won't that be crushing?" Sandy gave Qwilleran an adoring look. "Are you going to ask me to dance? Cal is a terrible dancer. He thinks he's a killer, but he's really a clod on the dance floor."

"Can you dance in that costume?"

Sandy's stiff white kimono was bound about the middle with a wide black obi. More white silk was draped over her straight dark hair.

"Oh, sure." She squeezed Qwilleran's arm as they walked to the dance floor. "Do you know what my costume represents?"

Qwilleran said no.

"Cal's in a black kimono. We're the Young Lovers in a Snowy Landscape."

"Who are they?"

"Oh, *you* know. The famous print—by Harunobu."

"Sorry. I'm a dunce when it comes to art." Qwilleran felt he could be debonair about the admission because, at that moment, he was leading Sandy expertly through a fox-trot enhanced by a few Qwilleran flourishes.

"You're a fun dancer," she said. "It takes real coordination to fox-trot to a cha-cha. But we must do something about your art education. Would you like me to tutor you?"

"I don't know if I could afford you—on my salary," he said, and Sandy's laughter could be heard above the orchestra. "How about the little lady from the other newspaper? Is she an art expert?"

"Her husband was a camouflage artist in World War I," said Sandy. "I guess that makes her an expert."

"And who are the rest of the people at your table?"

"Riggs is a sculptor. He does stringy, emaciated things that are shown at the Lambreth Gallery. They look like grasshoppers. So does Riggs, when you come to think of it. The other couple, the Buchwalters, are supposed to be Picasso's famous pair of lovers. You can't tell they're in costume. They always dress like peasants." Sandy turned up her nicely tilted nose. "I can't stand *her*. She thinks she's such an egghead. Her husband teaches art at Penniman School, and he's having a one-man show at the Westside Gallery. He's a vegetable, but he does lovely water colors." Then she frowned. "I hope newspapermen aren't eggheads. When Cal told me to— Oh, well, never mind. I talk too much. Let's just dance."

Qwilleran lost his partner shortly after, when a surly young man cut in. He was wearing a torn T-shirt and had the manners of a hoodlum. The face was familiar.

Later, back at the table, Sandy said, "That was Tom, our houseboy. He's supposed to be Stanley what's-his-name from that Tennessee Williams play, and his date is around here somewhere, dressed in a pink negligee. Tom is a boor, but Cal thinks he has talent, and so he's putting the kid through art school. Cal does a lot of wonderful things. You're going to write an article about him, aren't you?"

"If I can collect enough material," said Qwilleran. "He's difficult to interview. Perhaps you could help me."

"I'd love it. Did you know Cal is chairman of the State Council on Art? I think he wants to be the first professional artist to make the White House. He'll probably get there, too. He lets *nothing* stop him." She paused and became thoughtful. "You ought to write an article about the old man at the next table."

"Who's he?"

"They call him Uncle Waldo. He's a retired butcher who paints animals. He never held a paintbrush until he was sixty-nine."

"Where have I heard that before?" Qwilleran said.

"Oh, sure, every senior citizen wants to be a Grandma Moses, but Uncle Waldo is really talented—even if Georgie doesn't think so."

"Who's Georgie?"

"You know Georgie—your precious art critic."

"I haven't met the man yet. What's he like?"

"He's a real stinker, that's what he's like. When he reviewed Uncle Waldo's one-man show, he was absolutely cruel."

"What did he say?"

"He said Uncle Waldo should go back to operating a meat market and leave the cows and bunny rabbits to kids, who draw them with more imagination and honesty. He said Uncle Waldo butchered more livestock on canvas than he ever did in the meat business. Everyone was furious! Lots of people wrote letters to the editor, but the poor old man took it hard and stopped painting. It was a crime! He used to paint very charming primitives. I understand his grandson, who's a truck driver, went to the newspaper office and threatened to beat up George Bonifield Mountclemens, and I don't blame him. Your critic is completely irresponsible."

"Has he ever reviewed your husband's work?" Qwilleran asked with his best expression of innocence.

Sandy shuddered. "He's written some vicious things about Cal—just because Cal is a commercial artist and successful. Mountclemens classifies commercial artists with house painters and paperhangers. Actually Cal can draw better than any of those arty blotch-and-dribble kids who call themselves Abstract Expressionists. Not one of them could draw a glass of water!"

Sandy frowned and fell silent, and Qwilleran said, "You're prettier when you smile."

She obliged with a burst of laughter. "Look! Isn't that a panic? Cal is dancing with Mark Antony."

Qwilleran followed her pointing finger to the dance floor, where Cal Halapay in black Japanese kimono was guiding a husky Roman warrior through a slow fox-trot. The face under Antony's helmet was bold-featured but soft.

"That's Butchy Bolton," said Sandy. "She teaches sculpture at the art school—welded metal and all that sort of thing. She and her roommate came as Antony and Cleopatra. Isn't that a scream? Butchy welded her own armor. It looks like a couple of truck fenders."

Qwilleran said, "The paper should have sent a photographer. We should be getting pictures of all this."

Sandy did some acrobatics with her eyebrows and said, "Zoe Lambreth was supposed to handle publicity for the ball, but I guess she's only good at getting publicity for herself."

"I'm going to phone the picture desk," said Qwilleran, "and see if they'll send over a man."

Half an hour later, Odd Bunsen, who was working the one-to-eleven shift, arrived with a 35-mm. reflex camera hanging around his neck and the usual cigar between his teeth.

Qwilleran met him in the foyer and said, "Be sure to get a good shot of Cal and Sandra Halapay."

Odd said, "You're telling me? They love to get their noodles in the paper."

"Try to get everybody in pairs. They're dressed up as famous lovers—Othello and Desdemona, Lolita and Humbert Humbert, Adam and Eve—"

"Cr-r-azy!" said Odd Bunsen as he readied his camera. "How long do you have to hang around here, Jim?"

"Just long enough to see who wins the costume prizes and phone something in to the desk."

"Why don't you meet me at the Press Club for a nightcap? I can quit after I print these."

34

Back at the Halapay table, Sandy introduced Qwilleran to an impressive woman in a beaded evening dress. "Mrs. Duxbury," Sandy explained, "is the most important collector in the city. You should write an article about her collection. It's eighteenth-century English—Gainsborough and Reynolds, you know."

Mrs. Duxbury said, "I'm not anxious to have my collection publicized, Mr. Qwilleran, unless it will help you personally in your new position. Frankly, I am overjoyed to welcome you among us."

Qwilleran bowed. "Thank you. It's a completely new field for me."

"I trust your presence here means that the *Daily Fluxion* has at last come to its senses and dropped Mountclemens."

"No," said Qwilleran, "we're simply expanding our coverage. Mountclemens will continue to write critical reviews."

"What a pity. We were all hoping the newspaper would dismiss that horrid man."

A fanfare of trumpets from the stage announced the presentation of costume prizes, and Sandy said to Qwilleran, "I've got to collect Cal for the judging and the grand march. Are you sure you won't stay longer?"

"Sorry, I have to file my copy, but don't forget you're going to help me write a profile on your husband."

"I'll phone you and invite myself to lunch," said Sandy, giving the newsman an affectionate hug. "It will be fun."

Qwilleran moved to the back of the room and jotted down names as the winners were announced, and he was looking for a telephone when a woman's voice—soft and low—said, "Aren't you the new man from the *Daily Fluxion*?"

His moustache tingled. Women's voices sometimes affected him that way, and this voice was like caressing fingers.

"I'm Zoe Lambreth," she said, "and I'm afraid I failed miserably in my assignment. I was supposed to notify the newspapers about this ball, and it slipped my mind completely. I'm getting ready for a one-man show and working awfully hard—if you'll accept a lame excuse. I hope you're not being neglected. Are you getting all the information you need?"

"I think so. Mrs. Halapay has been looking after me."

"Yes, I noticed," Zoe said with a slight tightening of well-shaped lips.

"Mrs. Halapay was very helpful."

Zoe's eyebrows flickered. "I daresay."

"You're not in costume, Mrs. Lambreth."

"No. My husband didn't care to come tonight, and I just dropped in for a few minutes. I wish you would visit the Lambreth Gallery someday and meet my husband. Both of us would like to help you in any way we can."

"I'm going to need help. This is brand-new territory for me," Qwilleran said, and then slyly he added, "Mrs. Halapay has offered to supervise my art education."

"Oh, *dear!*" said Zoe with an intonation that suggested mild distress.

"Don't you approve?"

"Well . . . Sandra is not the most *knowledgeable* of authorities. Forgive me. Sooner or later you'll find out that artists are notorious cats." Zoe's large brown eyes were being disarmingly frank, and Qwilleran drowned in them momentarily. "But I'm really sincere in my concern for you," she went on. "I wouldn't want to see you—misdirected. Much of the work being produced today in the name of art is spurious at its worst and shoddy at its best. You should insist on knowing the credentials of your advisers."

"What would you suggest?"

"Come and visit the Lambreth Gallery," she urged, and her eyes echoed the invitation.

Qwilleran pulled in his waistline and entertained the idea of losing a few pounds—beginning tomorrow. Then he made another attempt to find a telephone.

The grand march was over, and the guests were circulating. Word had spread about the club that the *Daily Fluxion*'s new reporter was attending the party and that he was easily recognized by his prominent moustache. Consequently, numerous strangers approached Qwilleran and introduced themselves. Each one wished him well and followed with something uncomplimentary about George Bonifield Mountclemens. Those who were art dealers added brief commercials for their galleries; artists mentioned their forthcoming exhibitions; the laymen invited Qwilleran to come and see their private collections—anytime—and to bring a photographer if he wished.

Among those who hailed the newsman was Cal Halapay. "Come out to the house for dinner some evening," he said. "Bring the whole family."

Now the drinking commenced in earnest, and the party grew boisterous. The greatest commotion could be heard in the games room, and Qwilleran followed the crowd in that direction. He found the room packed with laughing guests, standing rib to rib with barely enough room to raise a highball glass, and the center of attention was Mark Antony. She was standing on a chair. Without a helmet Mark Antony was more nearly a woman—pudgy-faced, with a short haircut set in tight waves.

"Step right up, folks," she was barking. "Try your skill!"

Qwilleran squeezed into the room. The crowd, he discovered, was focusing its attention on a game of darts. Players were trying their aim at a life-size sketch of a man, chalked on

37

the barnwood wall with all features of the anatomy explicitly delineated.

"Step right up, folks," the woman warrior was chanting. "Doesn't cost a cent. One chance apiece. Who wants to play Kill the Critic?"

Qwilleran decided he had had enough. His moustache was feeling vaguely uncomfortable. He made a discreet exit, telephoned his story to the paper, and then joined Odd Bunsen at the Press Club.

"Mountclemens must be a pill," he said to the photographer. "Do you read his column?"

"Who reads?" said Odd. "I just look at the pictures and check my credit line."

"He seems to cause a lot of trouble. Do you know anything about the situation at the art museum?"

"I know they've got a cute chick in the checkroom," Odd said, "and some cr-r-razy nudes on the second floor."

"Interesting, but that's not what I mean. The museum just lost a million-dollar grant from some foundation, and the director was fired as a result. That's what I heard at the party tonight, and they say the whole ruckus was caused by the *Daily Fluxion's* critic."

"I wouldn't doubt it. He's always raising hell in the Photo Lab. He phones in and tells us what he wants photographed for his column. Then we have to go to the galleries to make the pix. You should see the garbage he expects us to photograph! Last week I went back to the Lambreth Gallery twice, and I still couldn't get a shot worth printing."

"How come?"

"The painting was black and navy blue, for Pete's sake! My print looked like a coal bin on a dark night, and the boss thought it was my fault. Old Monty's always beefing about our photographs. If I ever get a chance, I'd like to bust a speed graphic over his skull."

# CHAPTER FOUR

Sunday morning Qwilleran picked up a copy of the *Fluxion* at the hotel newsstand. He was living at an old, inexpensive hotel that had replaced its worn rugs and faded velvets with plastic floors and plastic-covered armchairs. In the coffee shop a countergirl in a plastic apron served his scrambled eggs on a cold plastic plate, and Qwilleran opened his newspaper to the art page.

George Bonifield Mountclemens III was reviewing the work of Franz Buchwalter. Qwilleran remembered the name. Buchwalter was the quiet man at the Halapay table—the husband of the social worker—the vegetable who painted lovely watercolors, in Sandy Halapay's estimation.

Two of the man's paintings had been photographed to illustrate the review, and Qwilleran thought they looked pretty good. They were sailboats. He had always liked sailboats. He began to read:

"Any gallery-goer who entertains an appreciation for fine craftsmanship must not miss Franz Buchwalter's one-man show at the Westside Gallery this month," wrote Mountclemens. "The artist, who is a watercolorist and instructor at

Penniman School of Fine Art, has elected to exhibit an outstanding collection of picture frames.

"It is obvious even to the untrained eye that the artist has been working diligently at his framing in the last year. The moldings are well-joined and the corners meticulously mitered.

"The collection is also distinguished by its variety. There are wide moldings, narrow moldings, and medium-size moldings, finished in gold leaf, silver leaf, walnut, cherry and ebony, as well as a murky wash intended to be that fashionable counterfeit known as antique white.

"One of the best frames in the show is a wormy chestnut. It is difficult for an observer to determine—without actually inserting a darning needle in the holes—whether this was manufactured by worms in North Carolina or by electric drills in Kansas City. However, a picture-framer of Buchwalter's integrity would be unlikely to use inferior materials, and this critic rather feels that it is genuine wormy chestnut.

"The exhibition is well hung. And special praise must be given to the matting, the textures and tones of which are selected with taste and imagination. The artist has filled his remarkable picture frames with sailboats and other subjects that do not detract from the excellence of the moldings."

Qwilleran looked at the illustrations again, and his moustache made small mute protests. The sailboats were pleasant —very pleasant indeed.

He gathered up his newspaper and left. He was about to try something he had not done since the age of eleven, and at that time he had been under duress. In short, he spent the afternoon at the art museum.

The city's art collection was housed in a marble edifice copied from a Greek temple, an Italian villa and a French chateau. In the Sunday sun it gleamed white and proud, sparkling with a fringe of dripping icicles.

He resisted an urge to go directly to the second floor for a look at the nudes recommended by Odd Bunsen, but he wandered into the checkroom for a glimpse of the cute chick. He found a long-haired, dreamy-faced girl wrestling with the coat hangers.

She said, glancing at his moustache, "Didn't I see you at the Turp and Chisel last night?"

"Didn't I see you in a pink negligee?"

"We won a prize—Tom LaBlanc and I."

"I know. It was a nice party."

"Real cool. I thought it would be a bomb."

In the lobby Qwilleran approached a uniformed attendant who wore the typical museum-guard expression of suspicion, disapproval and ferocity.

"Where can I find the museum director?" Qwilleran asked.

"He's not around on Sundays—as a rule—but I saw him walking through the lobby a minute ago. Probably came in to pack. He's leaving here, you know."

"Too bad. I hear he was a good man."

The guard wagged his head sympathetically. "Politics! And that muckraker down at the newspaper. That's what did it. I'm glad I'm civil service. . . . If you want to see Mr. Farhar, try his office—down this corridor and turn left."

The office wing of the museum was shrouded in its Sunday quiet. Noel Farhar, Director—according to the lettering on the door—was there alone.

Qwilleran walked through the unattended anteroom and into a paneled office adorned with art objects. "Excuse me," he said. "Mr. Farhar?"

The man rummaging in a desk drawer jumped back in a spasm of guilty acknowledgment. A more fragile young man Qwilleran had never seen. Although Noel Farhar seemed young for the job, his unhealthy thinness gave him a ghostly look of old age.

"Sorry to intrude. I'm Jim Qwilleran from the *Daily Fluxion.*"

Noel Farhar's clenched jaw was all too obvious, and he was unable to control the tremor that afflicted one eyelid. "What do you want?" he demanded.

Amiably Qwilleran said, "Just wanted to introduce myself. I'm new on the art beat and trying to get acquainted." He extended a hand and received a reluctant, trembling hand from Farhar.

"If they added you to the staff to mend matters," the director said coldly, "it's too late. The damage is done."

"I'm afraid I don't understand. I've just arrived in this city."

"Sit down, Mr. Qwilleran." Farhar folded his arms and remained standing. "I presume you know the museum has just lost a million-dollar grant."

"I heard about it."

"That would have given us the incentive and the prestige to raise another five million from private donors and industry. It would have given us the country's outstanding pre-Hispanic Mexican collection and a new wing to house it, but *your newspaper* subverted the entire program. *Your critic,* by his continual harassment and ridicule, presented this museum in such an unfavorable light that the Foundation withdrew its consideration." Farhar spoke forcefully despite his visible trembling. "Needless to say, this failure—plus Mount-clemens' personal attacks on my administration—has forced me to offer my resignation."

Qwilleran mumbled, "That's a serious charge."

"It is incredible that a single individual who knows nothing about art can pollute the city's art climate. But there's nothing you can do about it. I'm wasting my time talking to you. I have written to your publisher, demanding that this Mount-clemens be stopped before he destroys our cultural heritage."

Farhar turned back to the files. "Now I have some work to do—some papers to organize—"

"Sorry to interrupt," said Qwilleran. "Very sorry about this whole business. Not knowing the facts, I can't comment—"

"I've told you the facts." Farhar's tone put an end to the interview.

Qwilleran wandered about several floors of the museum, but his mind was not on the Renoirs and the Canalettos. The Toltec and Aztec cultures failed to capture his interest. Only the historic weapons stirred his enthusiasm—the left-handed daggers, German hunting knives, spiked maces, Spanish stylets and rapiers, Italian poniards. And repeatedly his thoughts went to the art critic that everyone hated.

Early the next morning Qwilleran was on the job at the *Fluxion*. In the reference library on the third floor he asked for the file of Mountclemens' reviews.

"Here it is," said the library clerk with a half-wink, "and when you finish with it, you'll find the first-aid room on the fifth floor—in case you need a bromo."

Qwilleran scanned twelve months of art reviews. He found the blistering appraisal of Cal Halapay's curly-haired kids ("drugstore art") and the cruel words about Uncle Waldo's primitives ("age is no substitute for talent"). There was a column, without mention of names, on private collectors who are less dedicated to art preservation than to tax avoidance.

Mountclemens had strong words to say about Butchy Bolton's life-size metal sculptures of the human figure, which reminded him of armor worn in a rural high-school performance of *Macbeth*. He deplored the mass production of third-rate artists at the Penniman School, whose assembly lines would do credit to a Detroit automobile factory.

He complimented the small suburban galleries for their role as afternoon social centers replacing the bridge club and the sewing circle, although he questioned their value as purveyors of art. And he inveighed against the museum: its policies, its permanent collection, its director, and the color of the uniforms worn by the guards.

Interspersed among the tirades, however, were the critic's enthusiastic endorsements of certain artists—especially Zoe Lambreth—but the jargon went over Qwilleran's head. "The complexity of eloquent dynamics in organic texture . . . internal subjective impulses expressed in compassionate linguistics."

There was also a column that had nothing to do with painting or sculpture but discussed cats (*Felis domestica*) as works of art.

Qwilleran returned the file to the library and looked up an address in the telephone book. He wanted to find out why Mountclemens thought Zoe Lambreth's work was so good—and why Cal Halapay thought it was so bad.

He found the Lambreth Gallery on the edge of the financial district, in an old loft building dwarfed by nearby office towers. It seemed to have class. The sign over the door was lettered in gold, and in the window there were only two paintings but thirty yards of gray velvet.

One of the canvases in the window was navy blue, sprinkled with black triangles. The other was a mysterious gravy of thick paint in tired browns and purples. Still, an image seemed to emerge from it, and Qwilleran felt a pair of eyes peering from its depths. As he stared, the expression in the eyes changed from innocence to awareness to savagery.

He opened the door and ventured inside. The gallery was long and narrow, furnished like a living room, rather richly, in uncompromising modern design. On an easel Qwilleran spotted another arrangement of triangles—gray scattered on white—which he preferred to the one in the window. The artist's signature was "Scrano." On a pedestal stood an elbow

44

of drain tile spiked with bicycle spokes. It was titled "Thing #17."

A bell had jangled somewhere when he entered the shop, and now Qwilleran heard footsteps tapping on the treads of the spiral staircase at the rear of the gallery. The iron structure, painted white, resembled a huge sculpture. Qwilleran saw feet, then narrow-trousered legs, and then the crisp, formal, supercilious proprietor of the gallery. It was hard for him to imagine Earl Lambreth as the husband of the warm, womanly Zoe. The man appeared somewhat older than his wife, and he was painfully dapper.

Qwilleran said, "I'm the new art reporter from the *Daily Fluxion*. Mrs. Lambreth asked me to visit your gallery."

The man did something that started to be a smile but ended as an unpleasant mannerism: he raked his bottom lip with his teeth. "Mrs. Lambreth mentioned you," he said, "and I suppose Mountclemens has told you that this is the leading gallery in the city. In fact, it is the *only* gallery worthy of the name."

"I haven't met Mountclemens as yet, but I understand he speaks highly of your wife's work. I'd like to see some of it."

The dealer, standing stiffly with hands behind his back, nodded toward a brown rectangle on the wall. "That is one of Mrs. Lambreth's recent paintings. It has the rich painterly quality recognized as her signature."

Qwilleran studied the picture in cautious silence. Its surface had the texture of a heavily iced chocolate cake, and he unconsciously passed his tongue over his lips. Yet he was aware, once more, of a pair of eyes somewhere in the swirls of paint. Gradually there evolved the face of a woman.

"She uses a lot of paint," Qwilleran observed. "Must take a long time to dry."

The dealer cleaned his lower lip again and said, "Mrs. Lambreth employs pigment to capture the viewer and en-

mesh him sensually before making her statement. Her decla-
mation is always elusive, nebulous—forcing her audience to
participate vitally in the interpretation."

Qwilleran nodded vaguely.

"She is a great humanist," Lambreth continued. "Unfortunately we have very few of her canvases here at present. She is
holding everything back for her one-man show in March.
However, you saw one of her most lucid and disciplined works
in the window."

Qwilleran remembered the paint-clouded eyes he had seen
before entering the gallery—the eyes full of mystery and
malice. He said, "Does she always paint women like that?"

Lambreth jerked one shoulder. "Mrs. Lambreth never
paints to formula. She has great versatility and imagination.
And the painting in the window is not intended to invoke
human associations. It is a study of a cat."

"Oh," said Qwilleran.

"Are you interested in Scrano? He is one of the foremost
contemporary artists. You saw one of his paintings in the
window. Here is another on the easel."

Qwilleran squinted at the gray triangles on a white background. The painted surface was fine-grained and slick, with a
gleam that was almost metallic; the triangles were crisp.

The newsman said, "He seems to be hooked on triangles. If
you hung this one upside down, you'd have three sailboats in
a fog."

Lambreth said, "The symbolism should be obvious. In his
hard-edge paintings Scrano expresses succinctly the essential
libidinous, polygamous nature of Man. The painting in the
window is specifically incestuous."

"Well, I guess that clobbers my theory," Qwilleran said. "I
was hoping I'd discovered some sailboats. What does Mountclemens say about Scarno?"

"S-c-r-a-n-o," Lambreth corrected him. "In Scrano's work

Mountclemens finds an intellectual virility that transcends the lesser considerations of artistic expression and focuses on purity of concept and sublimation of medium."

"Pretty expensive, I suppose."

"A Scrano usually runs into five figures."

"Whoosh!" said Qwilleran. "How about some of these other artists?"

"They command considerably less."

"I don't see any price tags anywhere."

Lambreth straightened a picture or two. "A gallery of this caliber would hardly be expected to post prices like a supermarket. For our major exhibitions we print a catalog, but what you see today is merely an informal showing of our own group of artists."

"I was surprised to find you located in the financial district," Qwilleran said.

"Our most astute collectors are businessmen."

Qwilleran took a turn around the gallery and reserved comment. Many of the canvases presented drips and blobs of paint in screaming, explosive colors. Some were composed solely of wavy stripes. There was a six-by-eight-foot close-up of a gaping red maw, and Qwilleran recoiled instinctively. On a pedestal stood an egg-shaped ball of metal titled "Untitled." Some elongated shapes in reddish clay resembled grasshoppers, but certain bulges convinced Qwilleran that he was looking at underfed humans. Two pieces of scrap metal were labeled "Thing #14" and "Thing #20."

Qwilleran liked the furniture better: scooplike lounge chairs, sofas floated on delicate chromium steel bases, and low tables with white marble tops.

He said, "Do you have any paintings by Cal Halapay?"

Lambreth cringed. "You must be joking. We are not that kind of gallery."

"I thought Halapay's stuff was highly successful."

47

"It's easily sold to persons who have no taste," said the dealer, "but actually Halapay's stuff—as you aptly describe it—is nothing but commercial illustration rather presumptuously installed in a frame. It has no value as art. In fact, the man would be doing the public a favor if he would forget his pretensions and concentrate on the activity he does so well—making money. I have no quarrel with hobbyists who want to spend their Sunday afternoons pleasantly in front of an easel, but they should not pose as artists and degrade the public taste."

Qwilleran turned his attention to the spiral staircase. "Do you have another gallery upstairs?"

"Just my office and the framing shop. Would you like to see the framing shop? It might interest you more than the paintings and sculpture."

Lambreth led the way past a stock room, where paintings were stored in vertical slots, and up the stairs. In the framing shop there was a disarrayed workbench and a lingering aroma of glue or lacquer.

"Who makes your frames?" asked Qwilleran.

"A very talented craftsman. We offer the best workmanship and the largest selection of moldings in the city." Still standing stiffly with his hands clasped behind his back, Lambreth nodded at a molding on the workbench. "That one sells for $35 a linear foot."

Qwilleran's gaze wandered to a cluttered office adjoining the workroom. He stared at a painting of a dancer hung crookedly on the wall. A ballerina in a filmy blue garment was depicted in a moment of arrested motion—against a background of green foliage.

"Now there's something I can understand," he said. "I really go for that."

"And well you might! It's a Ghirotto, as you can see by the signature."

48

Qwilleran was impressed. "I saw a Ghirotto at the museum yesterday. This must be a valuable piece of art."

"It would be—if it were complete."

"You mean it isn't finished?"

Lambreth drew an impatient breath. "This is only half of the original canvas. The painting was damaged. I'm afraid I could not afford a Ghirotto in good condition."

Qwilleran then noticed a bulletin board well plastered with newspaper clippings. He said, "I see the *Daily Fluxion* gives you pretty good coverage."

"You have an excellent art column," said the dealer. "Mountclemens knows more about art than anyone else in the city—including the self-styled experts. And he has integrity—unimpeachable integrity."

"Hmm," said Qwilleran.

"You will no doubt hear Mountclemens denounced on all sides—because he is weeding out the quacks and elevating the standards of taste. Recently he did the city a great service by dislodging Farhar at the museum. A new regime will bring life back to that dying institution."

"But didn't they lose a juicy grant at the same time?"

Lambreth waved his hand. "Another year, another grant, and by that time the museum will merit it."

For the first time Qwilleran noticed the dealer's hands, their grimy nails out of keeping with his fastidious dress. The newsman said, "Mountclemens thinks well of Mrs. Lambreth's work, I've noticed."

"He has been very kind. Many people think he favors this gallery, but the truth is: we handle only the best artists."

"This guy who paints triangles—is he a local artist? I might like to get an interview."

Lambreth looked pained. "It is rather well-known that Scrano is a European. He has been a recluse—in Italy—for many years. For political reasons, I believe."

49

"How did you find out about him?"

"Mountclemens brought his work to our attention and put us in touch with the artist's American agent, for which we are grateful. We are Scrano's exclusive representative in the Midwest." He cleared his throat and said proudly, "Scrano's work has an intellectualized virility, a transcendent purity—"

"I won't take any more of your time," said Qwilleran. "It's almost noon, and I have a luncheon appointment."

Qwilleran left the Lambreth Gallery with several questions banging about in his head: How could you tell good art from bad art? Why did triangles get thumbs up while sailboats got thumbs down? If Mountclemens was as good as Lambreth said, and if the local art situation was so unhealthy, why did Mountclemens stay in this thankless environment? Was he really a missionary as Lambreth said? Or a monster, as everyone else implied?

Then one more question mark waved its curly tail. Was there really a man named George Bonifield Mountclemens?

At the Press Club, where he was meeting Arch Riker for lunch, Qwilleran said to the bartender, "Does the *Fluxion* art critic ever come in here?"

Bruno paused in wiping a glass. "I wish he did. I'd slip him a Mickey."

"Why? What's your complaint?"

"Only one thing," said Bruno. "He's against the whole human race." He leaned over the bar in a confidential manner. "I tell you he's out to ruin every artist in town. Look what he did to that poor old man, Uncle Waldo. And Franz Buchwalter in yesterday's paper! The only artists he likes are connected with the Lambreth Gallery. You'd think he owned it."

"Some people think he's a highly qualified authority."

"Some people think down is up." Then Bruno smiled wisely. "Just wait till he starts gunning for you, Mr. Qwilleran. As soon as Mountclemens finds out you're snooping around on his beat—" The bartender pulled an imaginary trigger.

"You seem to know a lot about the art situation here in town."

"Sure. I'm an artist myself. I do collage. I'd like you to look at it sometime and give me a critical opinion."

"I've just had this job two days," Qwilleran told him. "I don't even know what collage is."

Bruno gave him a patronizing smile. "It's a form of art. I soak labels off whiskey bottles, cut them in little pieces and paste them up to make presidential portraits. I'm working on Van Buren now. It would make a terrific one-man show." His expression changed to a chummy one. "Maybe you could help me line up a gallery. Do you think you could, like, pull a few strings?"

Qwilleran said, "I don't know if there's much acceptance for presidential portraits made out of whiskey labels, but I'll ask around. . . . Now how about the usual—on the rocks?"

"One of these days," said the bartender, "you'll get hives from all this tomato juice."

When Arch Riker arrived at the bar, he found the art writer chewing his moustache. Arch said, "How did everything go this morning?"

"Fine," said Qwilleran. "At first I was slightly confused about the difference between good art and bad art, but now I'm completely confused." He took a swallow of tomato juice. "However, I've reached a conclusion about George Bonifield Mountclemens III."

"Let's have it."

"He's a fake."

"What do you mean?"

"He doesn't exist. He's a legend, an invention, a concept, a corporation, a gleam in the publisher's eye."

Arch said, "Who do you think writes all that copy we print under his sesquipedalian by-line?"

"A committee of ghost-writers. A committee of three. Probably a Mr. George, a Mr. Bonifield, and a Mr. Mountclemens. No one man could cause so much trouble, or be so hated, or have such an ambiguous image."

"You just don't know about critics, that's all. You're used to cops and robbers."

"I have an alternate theory, if you don't buy my first one."

"What's that?"

"It's a phenomenon of the electronics age. The art column is turned out by a battery of computers in Rochester, N.Y."

"What did Bruno put in your tomato juice?" Arch said.

"Well, I'm telling you one thing: I won't believe George Bonifield Mountclemens until I see him."

"All right. How about tomorrow or Wednesday? He's been out of town, but he's back now. We'll line up an appointment for you."

"Let's make it for lunch—here. We can eat upstairs—off a tablecloth."

Arch shook his head. "He won't come to the Press Club. He never comes downtown. You'll probably have to go to his apartment."

"Okay, line it up," said Qwilleran, "and maybe I'll take Bruno's advice and rent a bulletproof vest."

# CHAPTER FIVE

Qwilleran spent Tuesday morning at the Board of Education Building, viewing an exhibition of school children's art. He hoped to write something tenderly humorous about the crayoned sailboats floating in the sky, the purple houses with green chimneys, the blue horses that looked like sheep, and the cats—cats—cats.

After his venture into the uncomplicated world of juvenile art, Qwilleran returned to the office in a state of contented detachment. His arrival in the Feature Department caused an unnatural silence. Typewriters stopped chattering. Heads that had been bent over proofs were suddenly raised. Even the green telephones were respectfully quiet.

Arch said, "We've got news for you, Jim. We called Mountclemens to make an appointment for you, and he wants you to go tomorrow night. To *dinner!*"

"Huh?"

"Aren't you going to faint? The rest of the department did."

"I can see the headline now," said Qwilleran. "*Critic Poisons Reporter's Soup.*"

"He's supposed to be a great cook," Arch said. "A real

gourmet. If you're lucky, he'll postpone the arsenic until dessert. Here's his address."

At six o'clock Wednesday night Qwilleran took a cab to 26 Blenheim Place. The address was in an old section of town, once a fashionable neighborhood of stately homes. Most of them had become cheap rooming houses or quarters for odd business enterprises. There was a mender of antique porcelain, for example; Qwilleran guessed he was a bookie. Next door was an old coin shop, probably a front for a dope ring. As for the manufacturer of burlesque costumes, there was no doubt in Qwilleran's mind as to the real nature of that establishment.

In the midst of it all, one proud and plucky town house was making a last stand. It had a respectable residential air. It was tall for its width and primly Victorian, even to the ornamental iron fence. This was No. 26.

Qwilleran dodged a pair of neighborhood drunks careening down the sidewalk and walked up the stone steps to the small portico, where three mailboxes indicated the building had been made into apartments.

He smoothed his moustache, which was lively with curiosity and anticipation, and rang the bell. A buzzer unlocked the front door, and he walked into a tile-floored vestibule. Before him was another door, also locked—until a buzzer of another tone released it.

Qwilleran stepped into a palatial but dimly lighted entrance hall that enveloped him with its furnishings. He was aware of large gilt picture frames, mirrors, statuary, a table supported by gold lions, a carved bench like a church pew. Red carpet covered the hall floor and the stairway, and from the top of the flight came a voice with a finely honed edge:

"Come right up, Mr. Qwilleran."

The man at the top of the stairs was excessively tall and elegantly slender. Mountclemens wore a dark red velvet jacket, and his face impressed the newsman as poetic; perhaps it was the way the thin hair was combed down on the high forehead. A fragrance of lime peel surrounded him.

"Apologies for the moat-and-drawbridge arrangement downstairs," said the critic. "In this neighborhood one takes no chances."

He gave Qwilleran a left-handed handshake and ushered him into a living room unlike anything the newsman had ever seen. It was crowded and shadowy. The only illumination came from a flagging blaze in the fireplace and from hidden spotlights beamed on works of art. Qwilleran's eye itemized marble busts, Chinese vases, many gilded picture frames, a bronze warrior and some crumbling wood carvings of angels. One wall of the high-ceilinged room was covered with a tapestry having life-size figures of medieval damsels. Over the fireplace was a painting that any moviegoer would recognize as a Van Gogh.

"You seem impressed by my little collection, Mr. Qwilleran," said the critic, "or appalled by my eclectic taste. . . . Here, let me take your coat."

"It's a pocket-size museum," said Qwilleran in awe.

"It is my life, Mr. Qwilleran. And I admit—quite without modesty—that it succeeds in having a certain *ambiance*."

Hardly an inch of dark red wall remained uncovered. The fireplace was flanked by well-stocked bookshelves. Other walls were stacked to the ceiling with paintings.

Even the red carpet, which had a luminosity of its own, was crowded—with oversize chairs, tables, pedestals, a desk, and a lighted cabinet filled with small carvings.

"Let me pour you an apéritif," said Mountclemens, "and then you can collapse into an easy chair and prop your feet up. I avoid serving anything stronger than sherry or Dubonnet before dinner, because I am rather proud of my culinary skill, and I prefer not to paralyze your taste buds."

"I can't have alcohol," said Qwilleran, "so my taste buds are always in first-class condition."

"Then how about a lemon and bitters?"

While Mountclemens was out of the room, Qwilleran became aware of other details: a dictating machine on the desk; music drifting from behind an Oriental screen; two deep-cushioned lounge chairs facing each other in front of the fire, sharing a plump ottoman between them. He tried one of the chairs and was swallowed up in the cushions. Resting his head back and putting his feet on the ottoman, he experienced an unholy kind of comfort. He almost hoped Mountclemens would never return with the lemon and bitters.

"Is the music satisfactory?" asked the critic, as he placed a tray at Qwilleran's elbow. "I find Debussy soothing at this time of day. Here is something salty to nibble with your drink. I see you have gravitated to the right chair."

"This chair is the next best thing to being unconscious," said Qwilleran. "What's it covered with? It reminds me of something they used to make boys' kneepants out of."

"Heather corduroy," said Mountclemens. "A miracle fabric not yet discovered by scientists. Their preoccupation with man-made materials amounts to blasphemy."

"I'm living in a hotel where everything is plastic. It makes an old flesh-and-blood character like me feel obsolete."

"As you can see, by looking around you, I ignore modern technology."

"I'm surprised," said Qwilleran. "In your reviews you favor modern art, and yet everything here is—" He couldn't think of a word that sounded complimentary.

"I beg to correct you," said Mountclemens. He gestured grandly toward a pair of louvered doors. "In that closet is a small fortune in twentieth-century art—under ideal conditions of temperature and humidity. Those are my investments, but these paintings you see on the walls are my friends. I believe in the art of today as an expression of its time, but I choose to live with the mellowness of the past. For the same reason I am attempting to preserve this fine old house."

Mountclemens—sitting there in his velvet jacket, with Italian pumps on his long narrow feet and a dark red apéritif in his long white fingers—looked smug, sure, safe and unreal. His nasal voice, the music, the comfortable chair, the warmth of the fire and the dimness of the room were making Qwilleran drowsy. He needed action.

"Mind if I smoke?" he said.

"Cigarettes in that cloisonné box at your elbow."

"I use a pipe." Qwilleran searched for his quarter-bend bulldog and his tobacco pouch and his matches and commenced the ritual of lighting up.

As the flame from his match flared in the darkened room, he jerked his head to the side. He stared at the bookshelves. He saw a red light. It was like a signal. No, it was two red lights. Blazing red—and alive!

Qwilleran gasped. The rush of breath extinguished the match, and the red signals disappeared.

"What was—*that*? he said, when he stopped spluttering. "Something between the books. Something—"

"It was only the cat," said Mountclemens. "He likes to retire behind the books. The shelves are unusually deep because of my art books, and he can find a sanctum back there. Apparently he has had his afternoon nap behind the biographies. He seems to favor biographies."

"I never saw a cat with blazing red eyes," said Qwilleran.

"You will find that characteristic of Siamese cats. Shine a light in their eyes, and they turn ruby red. Ordinarily they are blue—like the blue in that Van Gogh. See for yourself when the cat decides to flatter us with his presence. For the moment he prefers seclusion. He is busy sensing you. Already he knows several things about you."

"What does he know?" Qwilleran squirmed in his chair.

"Having observed you, he knows you are unlikely to make any loud noises or sudden movements, and that is in your favor. So is your pipe. He likes pipes, and he knew that you smoked one, even before you extracted it from your pocket. He also realizes you are affiliated with a newspaper."

"How does he figure that?"

"Ink. He has quite a nose for printer's ink."

"Anything else?"

"At this moment he is flashing a message. He is telling me to serve the first course, or he will not get his own dinner until midnight."

Mountclemens left the room and returned with a tray of hot tarts.

"If you have no objection," he said, "we shall have the first course in the parlor. I have no servants, and you must forgive me if I employ a few informalities."

The crust was flaky; the filling was a tender custard flecked with cheese and spinach. Qwilleran savored every mouthful.

"You may wonder," said the critic, "why I prefer to manage without servants. I have a morbid fear of robbery, and I want no strangers coming to the house and discovering the valuables I keep on the premises. Please be good enough not to mention my collection downtown."

"Certainly—if that's the way you feel."

"I know how you newspaper people function. You are purveyors of news by instinct and by habit."

"You mean we're a bunch of gossips," said Qwilleran amiably, enjoying the last forkful of cheese custard and wondering what would come next.

"Let us simply say that a great deal of information—correct

and otherwise—is exchanged over the tables at the Press Club. Nevertheless, I feel I can trust you."

"Thank you."

"What a pity you don't drink wine. I had planned to celebrate this occasion by opening a bottle of Chateau Clos d'Estournel '45. It was a great vintage—very slow in maturing —even better than the '28's."

"Open it anyway," Qwilleran said. "I'll enjoy watching you enjoy it. Honestly!"

Mountclemens' eyes sparkled. "I need no further encouragement. And I shall pour you a glass of Catawba grape juice. I keep it in the house for—him."

"Who?"

"Kao K'o-Kung."

Qwilleran's face went momentarily blank.

"The cat," said Mountclemens. "Forgive me for forgetting you have not been formally introduced. He is very fond of grape juice, especially the white. And nothing but the best brand. He is a connoisseur."

"He sounds like quite a cat," Qwilleran said.

"A remarkable creature. He has cultivated an appreciation for certain periods of art, and although I disagree with his choice, I admire his independence. He also reads newspaper headlines, as you will see when the late edition is delivered. And now I believe we are ready for the soup." The critic drew aside some dark red velvet curtains.

An aroma of lobster greeted Qwilleran in the dining alcove. Plates of soup, thicky and creamy, were placed on a bare table that looked hundreds of years old. Thick candles burned in iron holders.

As he seated himself in a lavishly carved, high-backed chair, he heard a thud in the living room. It was followed by throaty mutterings. A floorboard creaked, and a light-colored cat with a dark face and slanting eyes walked into the dining alcove.

59

"This is Kao K'o-Kung," said Mountclemens. "He was named after a thirteenth-century artist, and he himself has the dignity and grace of Chinese art."

Kao K'o-Kung stood motionless and looked at Qwilleran. Qwilleran looked at Kao K'o-Kung. He saw a long, lean, muscular cat with sleek fur and an unbearable amount of assurance and authority.

Qwilleran said, "If he's thinking what I think he's thinking, I'd better leave."

"He is only sensing you," said Mountclemens, "and he appears stern when he concentrates. He is sensing you with his eyes, ears, nose and whiskers. His findings from all four avenues of investigation will be relayed to a central point for evaluation and synthesis, and—depending upon the verdict—he may or may not accept you."

"Thanks," said Qwilleran.

"He is somewhat of a hermit and suspicious of outsiders."

The cat took his time and, when he had finished looking at the visitor, calmly and without visible effort rose in vertical flight to the top of a tall cabinet.

"Whoosh!" said Qwilleran. "Did you see that?"

On top of the cabinet Kao K'o-Kung arranged himself in an imperious posture and watched the scene below with intelligent interest.

"A seven-foot leap is not unusual for a Siamese," said Mountclemens. "Cats have many gifts that are denied humans, and yet we tend to rate them by human standards. To understand a cat, you must realize that he has his own gifts, his own viewpoint, even his own morality. A cat's lack of speech does not make him a lower animal. Cats have a contempt of speech. Why should they talk when they can communicate without words? They manage very well among themselves, and they patiently try to make their thoughts known to humans. But in order to read a cat, you must be relaxed and receptive."

The critic's manner was serious and scholarly.

"For the most part," he went on, "cats resort to pantomime when dealing with humans. Kao K'o-Kung uses a code which is not difficult to learn. He scratches objects to call attention. He sniffs to indicate suspicion. He rubs against ankles when he wants service, and he shows his teeth to express disapproval. He also has a catly way of thumbing his nose."

"That I've got to see."

"Very simple. When a cat, who is a picture of grace and beauty, suddenly rolls over in a hideous posture, contorts his face and scratches his ear, he is telling you, sir, to go to blazes!"

Mountclemens removed the soup plates and brought in a tureen of chicken in a dark and mysterious sauce. A piercing howl came from the top of the cabinet.

Qwilleran said, "You don't need an antenna to tune in that kind of message."

"The lack of an antenna in the human anatomy," said the critic, "impresses me as a vast oversight, a cosmic blunder. With some simple arrangement of feelers or whiskers, think what man might have achieved in communication and prognostication! What we call extrasensory perception is normal experience for a cat. He knows what you are thinking, what you are going to do, and where you have been. I would gladly trade one ear and one eye for a full set of cat's whiskers in good working condition."

Qwilleran put down his fork and wiped his moustache carefully with his napkin. "That's very interesting," he said. He coughed once or twice and then leaned toward his host. "Do you want to know something? I have a funny feeling about my moustache. I've never told this to anyone, but ever since I grew this set of lip whiskers I've had a weird idea that I'm more—more aware! Do you know what I mean?"

Mountclemens nodded encouragingly.

"It's something I wouldn't want to get around at the Press Club," Qwilleran said.

Mountclemens agreed.

"I seem to see things more clearly," said the newsman.

Mountclemens understood.

"Sometimes I seem to sense what's going to happen, and I turn up in the right place at the right time. It's uncanny."

"Kao K'o-Kung does the same thing."

A deep grumble came from the top of the cabinet, and the cat stood up, arched his back in a taut stretch, yawned widely, and jumped to the floor with a grunt and velvety thud.

"Watch this," said the critic. "In three or four minutes the doorbell will ring, and it will be the newspaper delivery. Right now the newsboy is riding his bicycle two blocks away, but Kao K'o-Kung knows he's on his way here."

The cat walked across the living room to the hall and waited at the top of the stairs. In a few minutes the doorbell rang.

Mountclemens said to Qwilleran, "Would you be good enough to pick up the newspaper downstairs? He likes to read it while the news is fresh. Meanwhile, I will toss the salad."

The cat waited on the top stair with a dignified display of interest while the newsman walked down to retrieve the paper that had been tossed on the front porch.

"Lay the paper on the floor," Mountclemens instructed him, "and Kao K'o-Kung will read the headlines."

The cat followed this procedure closely. His nose twitched with anticipation. His whiskers moved up and down twice. Then he lowered his head to the screamer head, which was printed in two-inch type, and touched each letter with his nose, tracing the words: DEBBAN RELLIK DAM.

Qwilleran said, "Does he always read backwards?"

"He reads from right to left," Mountclemens said. "By the way, I hope you like Caesar salad."

It was a man's salad, zesty and full of crunch. Then came a bittersweet chocolate dessert with a velvet texture, and Qwilleran felt miraculously in harmony with a world in which art critics could cook like French chefs and cats could read.

Later they had small cups of Turkish coffee in the living room, and Mountclemens said, "How are you enjoying your new milieu?"

"I'm meeting some interesting personalities."

"The artists in this city have more personality than talent, I regret to say."

"This Cal Halapay is a hard one to figure out."

"He is a charlatan," said Mountclemens. "His paintings belong in advertisements for shampoo. His wife is decorative, if she keeps her mouth shut, but unfortunately she finds this an impossible feat. He also has a houseboy or protégé—or whatever the charitable term may be—who has the insolence to want a retrospective exhibition of his life's work at the age of twenty-one. Have you met any other representatives of this city's remarkable art life?"

"Earl Lambreth. He seems to be—"

"There is a pathetic case. No talent whatever, but he hopes to reach the stars on his wife's apron strings. His one and only achievement has been to marry an artist. How he managed to win such an attractive woman is beyond my imagination."

"She's good-looking, all right," Qwilleran agreed.

"And an excellent artist, although she needs to clean up her palette. She has done some studies of Kao K'o-Kung, capturing all his mystery, magic, perversity, independence, playfulness, savagery and loyalty—in one pair of eyes."

"I met Mrs. Lambreth at the Turp and Chisel last weekend. There was a party—"

"Are those aging adolescents still dressing up in fancy costumes?"

"It was a Valentine party. They all represented great lovers. First prize went to a woman sculptor called Butchy Bolton. You know her?"

"Yes," said the critic, "and good taste prevents me from making any comment whatever. I suppose Madame Duxbury was also there, dripping with sables and Gainsboroughs."

Qwilleran got out his pipe and took a long time lighting it. Then Kao K'o-Kung walked into the room from the direction of the kitchen and performed his after-dinner ritual for all to admire. In studious concentration he darted his long pink tongue over his face. Next he licked his right paw *well* and used it to wash his right ear. Then he changed paws and repeated the identical process on the left: one pass over the whiskers, one pass over the cheekbone, twice over the eye, once over the brow, once over the ear, once over the back of the head.

Mountclemens said to Qwilleran, "You may feel complimented. When a cat washes up in front of you, he is admitting you into his world. . . . Where are you planning to live?"

"I want to find a furnished apartment as soon as possible—anything to get sprung from that plastic-coated hotel."

"I have a vacancy downstairs," said Mountclemens. "Small but adequate—and furnished rather well. It has a gas fireplace and some of my second-best Impressionists. The rent would be insignificant. My chief interest is to have the place occupied."

"Sounds good," said Qwilleran from the depths of his lounge chair, with memories of Caesar salad and lobster bisque still soothing him.

"I travel a great deal, viewing exhibitions and serving on art juries, and in this dubious neighborhood it is a good idea to have signs of life in the front apartment downstairs."

"I'd like to have a look at it."

"Regardless of rumors that I am a monster," said Mountclemens in his most agreeable tone, "you will not find me a bad landlord. Everyone hates a critic, you know, and I imagine the gossips have described me as a sort of cultivated Beelzebub with artistic pretensions. I have few friends and, thankfully, no relatives, with the exception of a sister in Milwaukee who refuses to disown me. I am somewhat of a recluse."

Qwilleran made an understanding gesture with his pipe.

"A critic cannot afford to mix with artists," Mountclemens went on, "and when you hold yourself aloof, you invite jealousy and hatred. All my friends are here in this room, and I care for nothing else. My only ambition is to own works of art. I am never satisfied. Let me show you my latest acquisition. Did you know that Renoir painted window shades at one time in his career?" The critic leaned forward and lowered his voice, and a peculiar elation shone in his face. "I have two window shades painted by Renoir."

A shrill howl came from Kao K'o-Kung, who was sitting in a tall, compact posture, gazing into the fire. It was a Siamese comment that Qwilleran could not translate. More than anything else it sounded like a portent.

# CHAPTER SIX

On Thursday the *Daily Fluxion* published Qwilleran's first profile of an artist. His subject was Uncle Waldo, the elderly primitive and portrayer of livestock. Qwilleran had carefully avoided comment on the old man's artistic talent, building his story instead around the butcher's personal philosophy after a lifetime of selling chuck roasts to housewives in a lower-middle-class neighborhood.

The appearance of the story revived interest in Uncle Waldo's pictures, and on Friday the unimportant gallery that handled his work sold all their dusty canvases of beef cattle and woolly lambs and urged the old man to resume painting. Readers wrote to the editor commending Qwilleran's handling of the story. And Uncle Waldo's grandson, the truck driver, went to the offices of the *Daily Fluxion* with a gift for Qwilleran—ten pounds of homemade sausage that the retired butcher had made in his basement.

Friday evening Qwilleran himself was accorded some attention at the Press Club as he distributed links of knackwurst. He met Arch Riker and Odd Bunsen at the bar and ordered his usual tomato juice.

Arch said, "You must be quite a connoisseur of that stuff."

Qwilleran ran the glass under his nose and considered the bouquet thoughtfully. "An unpretentious vintage," he said. "Nothing memorable, but it has a naive charm. Unfortunately the bouquet is masked by the smoke from Mr. Bunsen's cigar. I would guess the tomatoes came from—" (he took a sip and rolled it on his tongue) "from Northern Illinois. Obviously a tomato patch near an irrigation ditch, getting the morning sun from the east and the afternoon sun from the west." He took another swallow. "My palate tells me the tomatoes were picked early in the day—on a Tuesday or Wednesday—by a farmhand wearing a Band-Aid. The Mercurochrome comes through in the aftertaste."

"You're in a good mood," said Arch.

"Yep," said Qwilleran. "I'm moving out of the plastic palace. I'm going to rent an apartment from Mountclemens."

Arch set his glass down with a thud of astonishment, and Odd Bunsen choked on cigar smoke.

"A furnished apartment on the first floor. Very comfortable. And the rent is only $50 a month."

"Fifty! What's the catch?" said Odd.

"No catch. He just doesn't want the house standing empty when he's out of town."

"There's gotta be a catch," Odd insisted. "Old Monty's too tightfisted to give anything away. Sure he doesn't expect you to be a cat-sitter when he's out of town?"

"Quit being a cynical press photographer," said Qwilleran. "Don't you know it's an outdated stereotype?"

Arch said, "Odd's right. When our messenger goes to pick up the tapes, Mountclemens sends him on all kinds of personal errands and never gives the kid a tip. Is it true he's got a houseful of valuable art?"

Qwilleran took a slow swallow of tomato juice. "He's got a lot of junk lying around, but who knows if it's worth anything?" He refrained from mentioning the Van Gogh. "The

67

big attraction is the cat. He's got a Chinese name—something like Koko. Mountclemens says cats like to hear a repetition of syllables when they're being addressed, and their ears are particularly receptive to palatal and velaric sounds."

"Somebody's nuts," said Odd.

"This cat is a Siamese, and he's got a voice like an ambulance siren. Know anything about the Siamese? It's a breed of supercat—very intelligent. This one can read."

"*Read?*"

"He reads newspaper headlines, but they have to be fresh off the press."

"What does this supercat think of my photographs?" Odd said.

"It's questionable whether cats can recognize pictorial images, according to Mountclemens, but he thinks a cat can sense the *content* of a picture. Koko prefers modern art to old masters. My theory is that the fresher paint gets through to his sense of smell. Same way with fresh ink on a newspaper."

"What's the house like?" Arch asked.

"Old. Declining neighborhood. But Mountclemens cherishes his place like a holy relic. They're tearing down buildings all around him, but he says he won't give up his house. It's quite a place. Chandeliers, elaborate woodwork, high ceilings —all carved plaster."

"Dust-catchers," said Odd.

"Mountclemens lives upstairs, and the downstairs is made into two apartments. I'm taking the front one. The rear is vacant, too. It's a nice quiet place except when the cat lets out a shriek."

"How was the food on Wednesday night?"

"When you taste Mountclemens' cooking, you forgive him for talking like a character in a Noel Coward play. I don't see how he turns out such dishes with his handicap."

"You mean his hand?"

"Yes. What's wrong with it?"

"That's an artificial hand he wears," said Arch.

"No kidding! It looks real, except for a little stiffness."

"That's why he tapes his column. He doesn't type."

Qwilleran thought about it for a few moments. Then he said, "I feel sorry for Mountclemens, in a way. He lives like a hermit. He thinks a critic shouldn't mix with artists, and yet art is his chief interest—that and the preservation of an old house."

"What did he say about the local art situation?" Arch asked.

"It's a funny thing. He didn't say much about art. We talked mostly about cats."

"See? What did I tell you?" said Odd. "Monty's lining you up for part-time cat-sitting. And don't expect a tip!"

The unseasonable weather, warm for February, ended that week. The temperature plunged, and Qwilleran bought a heavy pepper-and-salt tweed overcoat with his first full salary check.

For most of the weekend he stayed home, enjoying his new apartment. It had a living room with bed alcove, a kitchenette, and what Mountclemens would call *ambiance*. Qwilleran called it lots of junk. Still, he liked the effect. It was homey, and the chairs were comfortable, and there were gas logs in the fireplace. The picture over the mantel, according to the landlord, was one of Monet's less successful works.

Qwilleran's only complaint was the dim lighting. Light bulbs of low wattage seemed to be one of Mountclemens' economies. Qwilleran went shopping on Saturday morning and picked up some 75's and 100's.

He had a book from the library on how to understand modern art, and on Saturday afternoon he was coping with Dadaism in chapter nine, and chewing on a pipeful of unlighted tobacco, when an imperative wail sounded outside his door. Although it was clearly the voice of a Siamese cat, the cry was divided into syllables with well-placed emphasis, as if the command were "*Let* me *in!*"

Qwilleran found himself obeying the order punctually. He opened the door, and there stood Kao K'o-Kung.

For the first time Qwilleran saw the critic's cat in bright daylight, which streamed through the beveled glass windows of the hall. The light emphasized the luster of the pale fur, the richness of the dark brown face and ears, the uncanny blue of the eyes. Long brown legs, straight and slender, were deflected at the ends to make dainty feet, and the bold whiskers glinted with the prismatic colors of the rainbow. The angle of his ears, which he wore like a crown, accounted for his regal demeanor.

Kao K'o-Kung was no ordinary cat, and Qwilleran hardly knew how to address him. Sahib? Your Highness? On impulse he decided to treat the cat as an equal, so he merely said, "Won't you come in?" and stood aside, unaware that he was making a slight bow.

Kao K'o-Kung advanced to the threshold and surveyed the apartment carefully before accepting the invitation. This took some time. Then he stalked haughtily across the red carpet and made a routine inspection of the fireplace, the ashtray, the remains of some cheese and crackers on the table, Qwilleran's corduroy coat hanging on the back of a chair, the book on modern art, and an unidentified and almost invisible spot on the carpet. Finally satisfied with everything, he selected a place in the middle of the floor—at a carefully computed distance from the gas fire—and stretched out in a leonine pose.

"Can I get you something?" Qwilleran inquired.

The cat made no reply but looked at his host with a squeezing of the eyes that seemed to denote contentment.

"Koko, you're a very fine fellow," said Qwilleran. "Make yourself comfortable. Do you mind if I finish my reading?"

Kao K'o-Kung stayed half an hour, and Qwilleran relished the picture they made—a man, a pipe, a book, an expensive-looking cat—and he was disappointed when his guest arose, stretched, uttered a sharp adieu, and went upstairs to his own apartment.

Qwilleran spent the rest of the weekend anticipating his Monday lunch date with Sandra Halapay. He was circumventing the problem of interviewing her husband by writing a profile of Cal Halapay "through the eyes of his family and friends." Sandy was going to steer him to the right people, and she had promised to bring candid snapshots of her husband teaching the children to ski, feeding turkeys on the Oregon farm, and training a Kerry Blue to sit up.

All day Sunday Qwilleran felt that his moustache was transmitting messages to him—or perhaps it merely needed clipping. Just the same, its owner sensed that the coming week would be significant. Whether significantly good or significantly bad, the informed source did not reveal.

Monday morning arrived, and with it came an unexpected communication from upstairs.

Qwilleran was dressing and selecting a tie that Sandy might approve (a navy and green wool tartan, made in Scotland) when he first noticed the folded paper on the floor, half pushed under the door.

He picked it up. The handwriting was poor—like a child's scrawl—and the message was terse and abbreviated:

"Mr. Q—Pls del tapes to A.R. Save mess a trip—GBM."

Qwilleran had not seen his landlord since Friday evening. At that time he had moved his two suitcases from the hotel to the apartment and had paid a month's rent. A vague hope that Mountclemens would invite him to Sunday breakfast—

perhaps eggs Benedict or a chicken liver omelet—had evaporated. It appeared that only the cat was going to be sociable.

After deciphering the note, Qwilleran opened the door and found the reels of tape waiting for him on the hall floor. He delivered them to Arch Riker, but he thought the request strange—and unnecessary. The Dispatch Room at the *Fluxion* had a benchful of messengers who sat around pitching pennies most of the time.

Arch said, "Making any headway with the Halapay profile?"

"I'm taking Mrs. Halapay to lunch today. Will the *Flux* be willing to pick up the check?"

"Sure, they'll go for a couple of bucks."

"Where's a good place to take her? Somewhere special."

"Why don't you ask the Hungry Photographers? They're always getting people to buy lunch on expense accounts."

In the Photo Lab Qwilleran found six pairs of feet propped on desks, tables, wastebaskets and filing cabinets—waiting for assignments, or waiting for prints to come off the dryer, or waiting for the dark room buzzer.

Qwilleran said, "Where's a good place to take someone to lunch for an interview?"

"Who's paying?"

"The *Flux*."

"Sitting Bull's Chop House," the photographers said in unison.

"The chopped sirloin weighs a pound," said one.

"The cheese cake's four inches thick."

"They have a double lamb chop as big as my shoe."

It sounded good to Qwilleran.

Sitting Bull's Chop House was located in the packinghouse district, and a characteristic odor seeped into the dining room to compete with the cigar smoke.

"Oh, what a fun place," Sandy Halapay squealed. "How

clever of you to bring me here. So many *men!* I adore men."

The men adored Sandy, too. Her red hat topped with a proud black rooster tail was the center of attention. She ordered oysters, which the chop house could not supply, so she contented herself with champagne. But with each sip her laughter grew more shrill, rebounding from the antiseptic white tile walls of the restaurant, and the enthusiasm of her audience dwindled.

"Jim, dear, you must fly down to the Caribbean with me when Cal goes to Europe next week. I'll have the plane all to myself. Wouldn't it be *fun?*"

But she had forgotten to bring the information Qwilleran needed, and the snapshots of her husband were unusable. The lamb chop was indeed as big as a photographer's shoe and as flavorful. The waitresses, uniformed like registered nurses, were more efficient than cordial. The luncheon was not a success.

Back in the office that afternoon Qwilleran had to listen to telephone complaints about Mountclemens' review in Sunday's paper. The critic had called a watercolorist a frustrated interior decorator, and the watercolorist's friends and relatives were calling to castigate the *Daily Fluxion* and cancel their subscriptions.

Altogether Monday was not a halcyon day for Qwilleran. At the end of the tedious afternoon he fled to the Press Club for dinner, and Bruno, setting up a tomato juice, said, "I hear you've moved in with Mountclemens."

"I've rented one of his vacant apartments," Qwilleran snapped. "Anything wrong with that?"

"Not until he starts pushing you around, I guess."

Then Odd Bunsen stopped long enough to give the newsman an informed grin and say, "I hear old Monty's got you running errands for him already."

When Qwilleran returned home to 26 Blenheim Place, he

was in no mood for what he found. There was another note under his door.

"Mr. Q," it read, "Apprec pick up plane ticket—reserv Wed 3 P.M. NY—chg my acct—GBM."

Qwilleran's moustache bristled. It was true that the airline office was across the street from the *Daily Fluxion* Building, and picking up a plane ticket was a small favor for his landlord to ask in return for a good dinner. What irked him was the abruptness of the request. Or was it an order? Did Mountclemens think he was Qwilleran's boss?

Tomorrow was Tuesday. The plane reservation was for Wednesday. There was no time to make an issue of it, so Qwilleran grumbled to himself and picked up the ticket the following morning on his way to work.

Later in the day Odd Bunsen met him on the elevator and said, "Going away somewhere?"

"No. Why?"

"Saw you going into the airline office. Thought you were skipping town." He added a taunting grin. "Don't tell me you're running errands for Monty again!"

Qwilleran groomed his moustache with his knuckles and tried to reflect calmly that curiosity and a keen sense of observation make a good news photographer.

When he arrived home that evening, the third note was waiting under his door. It was more to his liking:

"Mr. Q—Pls bkfst w me Wed 8:30—GBM."

Wednesday morning Qwilleran went upstairs with the plane ticket and knocked on Mountclemens' door.

"Good morning, Mr. Qwilleran," said the critic, extending a thin white hand, his left. "I hope you are not in a hurry. I have a ramekin of eggs with herbs and sour cream, ready to put in the oven, if you can wait. And some chicken livers and bacon en brochette."

"For that I can wait," said Qwilleran.

"The table is set in the kitchen, and we can have a compote of fresh pineapple while we keep an eye on the broiler. I was fortunate enough to find a female pineapple at the market."

The critic was wearing silk trousers and a short Oriental coat tied with a sash around his remarkably thin midriff. There was a scent of lime peel. His thong sandals slapped as he led the way down a long hall to the kitchen.

The walls of the corridor were completely covered with tapestries, scrolls and framed pictures. Qwilleran remarked about the quantity.

"Also quality," said Mountclemens, tapping a group of drawings as he walked past them. "Rembrandt . . . Holbein. Very fine . . . Millet."

The kitchen was large, with three tall narrow windows. Bamboo blinds kept the light subdued, but Qwilleran peered through them and saw an exterior stairway—evidently a fire escape—leading down to a brick-walled patio. In the alley beyond the high wall he could see the top of a station wagon.

"Is that your car?" he asked.

"That grotesquery," said Mountclemens with an implied shudder, "belongs to the junk dealer across the alley. If I kept a car, it would have some felicity of design—a Karmann Ghia, or a Citroën. As it is, I dissipate my fortune in taxicabs."

The kitchen had a mellow clutter of antiques, copper utensils and clumps of dried vegetation.

"I dry my own herbs," Mountclemens explained. "Do you appreciate a little mint marinated with the pineapple? I think it gives the fruit another dimension. Pineapple can be a little too direct. I grow the mint in a pot on the windowsill—chiefly for Kao K'o-Kung. His idea of a choice plaything is a bouquet of dried mint leaves tied in the toe of a sock. In a moment of rare wit we have named his toy Mintie Mouse. A rather free abstraction of a mouse, but that is the sort of thing that appeals to his artistic intellect."

Mountclemens was putting individual baking dishes into the oven one at a time, using his left hand.

"Where is Koko this morning?" Qwilleran asked.

"You should be able to feel his gaze. He is watching you from the top of the refrigerator—the only down-cushioned refrigerator west of the Hudson River. It is his bed. He refuses to sleep anywhere else."

The aroma of bacon, herbs and coffee was beginning to swirl about the kitchen, and Koko—on a blue cushion that matched his eyes—raised his nose to sniff. So did Qwilleran.

He said, "What do you do about the cat when you go to New York?"

"Ah, that is the problem," said the critic. "He requires a certain amount of attention. Would it be an imposition if I asked you to prepare his meals while I am away? I'll be gone less than a week. He takes only two meals a day, and his diet is simple. There is raw beef in the refrigerator. You merely carve it in small pieces the size of a lima bean, put it in a pan with a little broth, and warm it gently. A dash of salt and a sprinkling of sage or thyme will be appreciated."

"Well—" said Qwilleran, spooning up the last of the minted pineapple juice.

"To make it easier for you in the mornings, when you are headed for the office, he could have a slice of *pâté de la maison* for breakfast instead of beef. It makes a welcome change for him. Would you like your coffee now or later?"

"Later," said Qwilleran. "No—I'll take it now."

"And then there is the matter of his commode."

"What's that?"

"His commode. You'll find it in the bathroom. It needs very little attention. He is an immaculate cat. You will find the sand for the commode in the Chinese tea chest at the foot of the bathtub. Do you take sugar or cream?"

"Black."

76

"If the weather is not too inclement, he can take a little exercise in the patio, provided you accompany him. Normally he gets sufficient exercise by running up and down the front stairs. I leave my apartment door ajar for his comings and goings. To be on the safe side, I shall also give you a key. Is there anything I can do for you in New York?"

Qwilleran had just experienced the first forkful of chicken livers rolled in bacon and seasoned with a touch of basil, and he rolled his eyes gratefully heavenward. In doing so, he caught the gaze of Kao K'o-Kung, perched on the refrigerator. The cat slowly and deliberately closed one eye in an unmistakable wink.

# CHAPTER SEVEN

"I have a complaint," Qwilleran told Arch at the Press Club on Wednesday night.

"I know what it is. Your name was spelled with a U yesterday, but we caught it in the second edition. You know what's going to happen, don't you? The next time the typographers' union meets with management, the spelling of your name is going to be one of their grievances."

"I have another beef, too. I wasn't hired to be an orderly for your art critic, but that's what he seems to think. Do you know he's leaving town tonight?"

"I guessed as much," said Arch. "That last batch of tapes included enough copy for three columns."

"First I delivered those tapes for him. And then I picked up his ticket for the three o'clock plane this afternoon. And now I'm expected to do latrine duty for his cat!"

"Wait till Odd Bunsen hears this!"

"Don't tell him! Nosy Bunsen will find out soon enough in his own devious way. I'm supposed to feed the cat twice a day, change his drinking water, and attend to his commode. Do you know what a commode is?"

"I can guess."

"It was new to me. I thought cats just ran out in the backyard."

"There's nothing in the Guild contract about reporters doing toidy service," Arch said. "Why didn't you decline?"

"Mountclemens didn't give me a chance. He's a sly operator! There I was, sitting in his kitchen, mesmerized by fresh pineapple, broiled chicken livers and eggs in sour cream. It was *female* pineapple, what's more. What could I do?"

"You'll have to choose between pride and gluttony, that's all. Don't you like cats?"

"Sure, I like animals, and this cat is more human than a few people I could name. But he gives me the uncomfortable feeling that he knows more than I do—and he's not telling what it is."

Arch said, "We have cats around the house all the time. The kids bring them home. But none of them ever gave me an inferiority complex."

"Your kids never brought home a Siamese."

"You can stand it for three or four days. If it gets too much for you, we'll send a copyboy with a master's degree. He should be able to cope with a Siamese."

"Knock it off. Here comes Odd Bunsen," said Qwilleran.

Even before the photographer appeared, the cigar could be detected and the voice could be heard, complaining about the frigid temperature outside.

Odd tapped Qwilleran on the shoulder. "Are those cat hairs on your lapel, or have you been dating a blonde with a crew cut?"

Qwilleran combed his moustache with a swizzle stick.

Odd said, "I'm still on nights. Any of you guys want to eat with me? I've got an hour for dinner, if nobody blows up City Hall."

"I'll eat with you," said Qwilleran.

They found a table and consulted the menu. Odd ordered

Salisbury steak, complimented the waitress on the trimness of her waistline, and then said to Qwilleran, "Well, have you got old Monty figured out yet? If I went around insulting everybody the way he does, I'd get fired—or assigned to Society, what's worse. How does he get away with it?"

"Critic's license. Besides, newspapers like controversial writers."

"And where does he get all his money? I hear he lives pretty well. Travels a lot. Drives an expensive car. He doesn't do that on what the *Flux* pays him."

"Mountclemens doesn't drive," Qwilleran said.

"Sure, he does. I've seen him behind the wheel. I saw him this morning."

"He told me he didn't have a car. He rides taxis."

"Maybe he doesn't own one, but he drives one sometimes."

"How do you suppose he manages?"

"No sweat. Automatic transmission. Didn't you ever do any one-arm driving? You must be a lousy lover. I used to drive with one arm, shift gears and eat a hot dog all at the same time."

"I've got a few questions, too," Qwilleran said. "Are the local artists as bad as Mountclemens says? Or is he as phony as the artists think? Mountclemens says Halapay is a charlatan. Halapay says Zoe Lambreth's paintings are a hoax. Zoe says Sandy Halapay is uninformed. Sandy says Mountclemens is irresponsible. Mountclemens says Farhar is incompetent. Farhar says Mountclemens knows nothing about art. Mountclemens says Earl Lambreth is pathetic. Lambreth says Mountclemens is a monument of taste, truth and integrity. So . . . who's on first?"

"Listen!" said Odd. "I think they're paging me."

The voice mumbling over the public-address system could hardly be heard above the hubbub in the bar.

"Yep, that's for me," the photographer said. "Somebody must have blown up the City Hall."

He went to the telephone, and Qwilleran pondered the complexities of the art beat.

When Odd Bunsen returned from the telephone booth, he was taut with excitement.

Qwilleran thought, A press photographer for fifteen years, and he still lights up when there's a three-alarm fire.

"I've got news for you," said Odd, leaning over the table and keeping his voice down.

"What is it?"

"Trouble on your beat."

"What kind of trouble?"

"Homicide! I'm on my way to the Lambreth Gallery."

"The Lambreth!" Qwilleran stood up fast enough to knock over his chair. "Who is it? . . . Not Zoe!"

"No. Her husband."

"Know what happened?"

"They said he was stabbed. Want to come with me? I told the desk you were here, and they said it would be good if you could cover it. Kendall's out on a story, and both leg men are busy."

"Okay, I'll go."

"Better phone them back and say so. I've got my car outside."

When Qwilleran and Bunsen arrived in front of the Lambreth Gallery, there was an unwarranted calm in the street. The financial district was normally deserted after five-thirty, and even a murder had failed to draw much of a crowd. A sharp wind whipped down the canyon created by nearby office buildings, and only a few shivering stragglers stood about on the sidewalk, but they soon moved on. A loneliness filled the street. Isolated voices sounded unreasonably loud.

The newsmen identified themselves to the patrolman at

the door. Inside, the expensive art and plush furnishings made an unlikely background for the assortment of uninvited guests. A police photographer was taking pictures of some paintings that had been viciously slashed. Bunsen pointed out the precinct inspector and Hames, a detective from the Homicide Bureau. Hames nodded at them and jerked a thumb upstairs.

The newsmen started up the spiral staircase at the rear and then backed away to let a fingerprint man come down. He was talking to himself. He was saying, "How can they get a stretcher down this thing? They'll have to take him out the window."

Upstairs a sharp voice was saying, "Come on, you fellows. You can take care of that downstairs. Let's thin out."

"That's Wojcik from Homicide," said Bunsen. "No fooling around with him."

The framing shop was approximately as Qwilleran remembered it—except for the men with badges, cameras and notebooks. A patrolman stood in the doorway to Lambreth's office, facing out. Over his shoulder Qwilleran could see that the office had been fairly well wrecked. The body lay on the floor near the desk.

He got Wojcik's attention and flipped open a small notebook. "Murderer known?"

"No," said the detective.

"Victim: Earl Lambreth, director of the gallery?"

"Right."

"Method?"

"Stabbed with a tool from the workbench. A sharp chisel."

"Where?"

"Throat. A very wet job."

"Body discovered where?"

"In his office."

"By whom?"

"Victim's wife, Zoe."

Qwilleran took a second to gulp and grimace.

"That's spelled Z-o-e," said the detective.

"I know. Any sign of a struggle?"

"Office practically turned upside down."

"What about the vandalism in the gallery?"

"Several pictures damaged. A statue broken. You can see that downstairs."

"What time did it happen?"

"The electric clock—knocked off the desk—stopped at six-fifteen."

"The gallery was closed at that time."

"Right."

"Any evidence of forcible breaking and entering?"

"No."

"Then the murderer could have been someone who had legitimate access to the place."

"Could be. We found the front door locked. The alley door may or may not have been locked when Mrs. Lambreth arrived."

"Anything stolen?"

"Not immediately apparent." Wojcik started to move away. "That's all. You've got the story."

"One more question. Any suspects?"

"No."

Downstairs, while Bunsen scrambled around taking pictures, Qwilleran studied the nature of the vandalism. Two oil paintings had been ripped diagonally by a sharp instrument. A framed picture lay on the floor with its glass broken, as if a heel had been put through it. A reddish clay sculpture appeared to have been bounced off a marble-top table; there were scattered fragments.

Paintings by Zoe Lambreth and Scrano—the only two names that registered with Qwilleran—were unharmed.

He remembered the sculpture from his previous visit. The elongated shape with random swellings had apparently been a woman's figure. Its label, still affixed to the empty pedestal, said, "*Eve* by B. H. Riggs—terra cotta."

The watercolor on the floor was one Qwilleran had not noticed the week before. It resembled a jigsaw puzzle of many colors—just a pleasing pattern. It was titled "Interior," and the artist's name was Mary Ore. The label called it a gouache.

Then Qwilleran examined the two oils. Both were composed of wavy vertical stripes of color, applied on a white background with a wide brush. The colors were violent—red, purple, orange, pink—and the paintings seemed to vibrate like a plucked string. Qwilleran wondered who would buy these nerveracking works of art. He preferred his second-rate Monet.

Stepping closer to check the labels, he noted that one was "Beach Scene # 3 by Milton Ore—oil," while the other was "Beach Scene #2" by the same artist. In a way the titles were a help in appreciating the pictures. They began to remind Qwilleran of shimmering heat waves rising from hot sand.

He said to Bunsen, "Look at these two pictures. Would you say they were beach scenes?"

"I'd say the artist was drunk," said Odd.

Qwilleran moved back a few paces and squinted at the two oils. Suddenly he saw a crowd of standing figures. He had been looking at the red, orange and purple stripes, and he should have been seeing the white voids between them. The vertical stripes of white suggested the contours of female bodies—abstract but recognizable.

He thought, "Women's figures in those white stripes . . . a woman's torso in the broken clay. Let's have another look at the watercolor."

When he knew what he was searching for, it was not hard

to find. In the jagged wedges of color that made up the pattern of Mary Ore's work, he could distinguish a window, a chair, a bed—on which reclined a human figure. Female.

He said to Odd Bunsen, "I'd like to go out to the Lambreth house and see if Zoe will talk to me. Also, she might have a photograph of the deceased. Shall we check with the desk?"

After phoning the details to a rewrite man and getting a go-ahead from the City Desk, Qwilleran folded himself into Odd Bunsen's cramped two-seater, and they drove to 3434 Sampler Street.

The Lambreth home was a contemporary town house in a new neighborhood—self-consciously well designed—that had replaced a former slum. The newsmen rang the doorbell and waited. Draperies were drawn to cover the large windows, but it could be seen that lights were burning in every room, upstairs and downstairs. They rang the bell again.

When the door opened, the trousered woman who stood there—arms folded belligerently, feet planted solidly on the threshold—looked familiar to Qwilleran. She was tall and husky. Her soft face was set in a stern expression.

"Yes?" she said defiantly.

"I'm a friend of Mrs. Lambreth," said Qwilleran. "I wonder if I could see her and offer my assistance. Jim Qwilleran's the name. This is Mr. Bunsen."

"You're from the paper. She's not going to see any reporters tonight."

"This isn't an official visit. We were on our way home and thought there might be something we could do. Aren't you Miss Bolton?"

Inside the house a low, tired voice called, "Who is it, Butchy?"

"Qwilleran and another man from the *Fluxion*."

"It's all right. Ask them in."

The newsmen stepped into a room furnished in stark contemporary style. The furnishings were few, but fine, and there—leaning against a doorjamb—was Zoe Lambreth wearing purple silk trousers and a lavender blouse and looking gaunt and bewildered.

Butchy said, "She should be lying down and resting."

Zoe said, "I'm all right. I'm too keyed up to do any resting."

"She wouldn't take a sedative."

"Will you gentlemen sit down?" Zoe said.

Qwilleran's face reflected the sympathetic understanding for which he was famous. Even his moustache contributed to the expression of grave concern. He said, "I don't need to tell you my feelings. Even though our acquaintance was short, I feel a personal loss."

"It's terrible. Just terrible." Zoe sat on the extreme edge of the sofa, with her hands folded on her knees.

"I visited the gallery last week, as you suggested."

"I know. Earl told me."

"It's impossible to imagine what a shock this must have been."

Butchy interrupted. "I don't think she should be talking about it."

"Butchy, I've got to talk about it," said Zoe, "or I'll go crazy." She looked at Qwilleran with the full brown eyes that he remembered so well from their first meeting, and now they reminded him of the eyes in Zoe's own paintings at the gallery.

He said, "Was it your custom to go to the gallery after it was closed?"

"Quite the contrary. I seldom went there at any time. It looks unprofessional for an artist to hang around the gallery that handles her work. Especially in our case—husband and wife. It would look too folksy!"

"The gallery impressed me as very sophisticated," Qwilleran said. "Very suitable for the financial district."

Butchy said, with a frank show of pride, "That was Zoe's idea."

"Mrs. Lambreth, what caused you to go to the gallery tonight?"

"I was there twice. The first time was just before closing time. I had been shopping all afternoon and stopped in to see if Earl wanted to stay downtown for dinner. He said he couldn't leave until seven o'clock or later."

"What time was it when you were talking to him?"

"The front door was still open, so it must have been before five-thirty."

"Did he explain why he couldn't leave the gallery?"

"He had to work on the books—for a tax deadline or something—so I went home. But I was tired and didn't feel like cooking."

Butchy said, "She's been working night and day, getting ready for a one-man show."

"So I decided to have a bath and change clothes," Zoe went on, "and go back downtown at seven o'clock and drag Earl away from his books."

"Did you telephone him to say you were returning to the gallery?"

"I think so. Or maybe I didn't. I can't remember. I thought about phoning, but in the rush of getting dressed, I don't know whether I called or not. . . . You know how it is. You do things automatically—without thinking. Sometimes I can't remember whether I've brushed my teeth, and I have to look at the toothbrush to see if it's wet."

"When did you arrive at the gallery the second time?"

"Just about seven o'clock, I think. Earl had taken the car in for repairs, so I called a taxi and had the driver take me to the alley entrance of the gallery. I have a key for the back door—just in case of emergency."

"It was locked?"

"That's another thing I don't remember. It should have been locked. I put my key in the lock and turned the door handle without thinking much about it. The door opened, and I went in."

"Did you notice anything amiss on the ground floor?"

"No. The lights were out. I went right up the spiral staircase. As soon as I walked into the workroom, I sensed something wrong. It was deadly quiet. I was almost afraid to go into the office." She was remembering it painfully. "But I did. First I saw—papers and everything all over the floor. And then—" She put her face in her hands, and there was silence in the room.

After a while Qwilleran said gently, "Would you like me to notify Mountclemens in New York? I know he thought highly of you both."

"If you wish."

"Have the funeral plans been made?"

Butchy said, "There won't be a funeral. Zoe doesn't approve of funerals."

Qwilleran stood up. "We'll be going now, but please let me know—Mrs. Lambreth—if there's anything I can do. Sometimes it helps just to talk."

Butchy said, "I'm here. I'm looking after her."

Qwilleran thought the woman sounded possessive. He said, "Just one more thing, Mrs. Lambreth. Do you have a good photograph of your husband?"

"No. Just a portrait I painted last year. It's in my studio. Butchy will show you. I think I'll go upstairs."

She walked from the room without further ceremony, and Butchy led the newsmen to the studio at the rear of the house.

88

There on the wall was Earl Lambreth—cold, haughty, supercilious—painted without love.

"Perfect likeness," said Butchy with pride. "She really captured his personality."

Almost inaudible was the click of Odd Bunsen's camera.

## CHAPTER EIGHT

When Qwilleran and Odd Bunsen drove away from the Lambreth house, they shivered in silence until the heater in Odd's car gave out the first promising puff.

Then Odd said, "The Lambreths seem to be doing all right at that art racket. Wish I could live like that. I'll bet that sofa was worth a thousand bucks. Who was that big bruiser?"

"Butchy Bolton. Teaches sculpture at Penniman School of Fine Art."

"She really thought she was running the show. Enjoying it, too."

Qwilleran agreed. "Butchy didn't strike me as being exactly grief-stricken over the loss of Earl Lambreth. I wonder where she fits into the picture. Friend of the family, I suppose."

"If you ask me," said Odd, "I don't think that doll Zoe was taking it too hard, either."

"She's a calm, intelligent woman," Qwilleran said, "even if she is a doll. She's not the type to collapse."

"If my wife ever finds me lying in a pool of blood, I want her to collapse and collapse good! I don't want her running home and fixing her lipstick and putting on a sharp outfit to receive callers. Imagine a dame not remembering whether she telephoned her husband or not, and not remembering whether the gallery door was locked!"

"It was the shock. It leaves blanks in the memory. She'll remember tomorrow—or the next day. What did you think of the portrait she painted of her husband?"

"Perfect! He's a cold fish. I couldn't have taken a photograph that was any better."

Qwilleran said, "I used to think these modern artists painted drips and blots because they couldn't draw, but now I'm not so sure. Zoe is really talented.

"If she's so talented, why does she waste her time painting that modern garbage?"

"Probably because it sells. By the way, I'd like to meet our police reporter."

"Lodge Kendall? Haven't you met him yet? He's over at the Press Club just about every day for lunch."

"I'd like to have a talk with him."

"Want me to line it up for tomorrow?" Odd said.

"Okay. . . . Where are you headed now?"

"Back to the Lab."

"If it isn't out of your way, would you drop me at my apartment?"

"No sweat."

Qwilleran looked at his wristwatch in the glow from the instrument panel. "It's ten-thirty!" he said. "And I forgot to feed the cat."

"A-hah! A-hah!" said Odd. "I told you Monty wanted you for a cat-sitter." A few minutes later, when he turned the car into Blenheim Place, he said, "Doesn't this neighborhood scare the hell out of you? The characters you see on the streets!"

"They don't bother me," said Qwilleran.

"You wouldn't get *me* to live here! I'm a coward."

A folded newspaper lay on the porch of No. 26. Qwilleran picked it up, unlocked the front door and closed it quickly behind him, glad to get in out of the cold. He rattled the door handle to make sure it was locked again—as Mountclemens had warned him to do.

Using a second key, he unlocked the inner vestibule door. And that's when he recoiled in black fright!

Out of the dark came a wild scream. Qwilleran's mind went blank. The hairs of his moustache stood on end. His heart pounded. Instinctively he gripped the newspaper like a club.

Then he realized the source of the scream. Koko was waiting for him. Koko was scolding him. Koko was hungry. Koko was furious.

Qwilleran leaned against the doorjamb and gasped. He loosened his tie.

"*Never* do that again!" he told the cat.

Koko was sitting on the table that was supported by golden lions, and he retorted with a torrent of abuse.

"All right! All right!" Qwilleran yelled at him. "I apologize. I forgot, that's all. Important business downtown."

Koko continued his tirade.

"Wait till I take my coat off, will you?"

Once Qwilleran started upstairs, the tumult ceased. The cat bounded ahead and led him into Mountclemens' apartment, which was in darkness. Qwilleran groped for a light switch. This delay irritated Koko, who commenced another vocal demonstration. Now the piercing cries had gravel-throated undertones signifying menace.

"I'm coming. I'm coming," said Qwilleran, following the cat down the long narrow hall to the kitchen. Koko led him directly to the refrigerator, where there was a chunk of beef waiting in a glass tray. It looked like a whole tenderloin.

Qwilleran put the meat on a built-in butcher's block and hunted for a sharp knife.

"Where does he keep his knives?" he said, pulling open one drawer after another.

Koko leaped lightly to the adjoining counter and nosed a knife rack, where five handsome blades hung point downward on a magnetized bar.

"Thanks," said Qwilleran. He started to carve the beef, marveling at the quality of the cutlery. Real chef's knives. They made meat-cutting a pleasure. How did Mountclemens say to cut the beef? The size of a kidney bean or the size of a navy bean? And how about the broth? He said to warm it in broth. Where was the broth?

The cat was sitting on the counter, supervising every move with what appeared to be an impatient scowl.

Qwilleran said, "How about eating it raw, old man? Since it's so late—"

Koko gargled a low note in his throat, which Qwilleran assumed was acquiesence. In a cupboard he found a plate—white porcelain with a wide gold band. He aranged the meat on it—attractively, he thought—and placed it on the floor alongside a ceramic water bowl decorated with the word "cat" in three languages.

Koko jumped to the floor with a grunt, walked to the plate and examined the beef. Then he looked up at Qwilleran with incredulity displayed in the tilt of his ears.

"Go ahead. Eat," said Qwilleran. "Enjoy it in good health."

Koko lowered his head once more. He sniffed. He touched the beef with his paw and gave a perceptible shudder. He shook his paw fastidiously and walked away, his tail pointed stiffly toward the North Star.

Later, after Qwilleran had found some thin gravy in the

93

refrigerator and prepared the meal properly, Kao K'o-Kung consented to dine.

The newsman related the experience at the Press Club the following noon when he had lunch with Arch Riker and Lodge Kendall.

"But this morning I acquitted myself admirably," said Qwilleran. "Koko got me up at six-thirty by yelling outside my door, and I went up and prepared breakfast to his satisfaction. I think he's going to let me keep the job until Mount-clemens comes home."

The police reporter was young, tense, earnest, literal and unsmiling. He said, "Do you mean to say you let a cat boss you around?"

"Actually, I feel sorry for him. Poor little rich cat! Nothing but tenderloin and *pâté de la maison*. I wish I could catch him a mouse."

Arch explained to Kendall, "You see, this is a Siamese, descended from an Egyptian god. It not only communicates and runs the show; it reads newspaper headlines. A cat that can read is obviously superior to a newspaperman who can't catch mice."

Qwilleran said, "He flies, too. When he wants to get to the top of an eight-foot bookcase, he just puts his ears back and zooms up like a jet. No wings. He's got some kind of aero-dynamic principle that ordinary cats don't have."

Kendall regarded the two older men with wonder and suspicion.

"After Koko got me up at six-thirty," said Qwilleran, "I started thinking about the Lambreth murder. Any developments, Lodge?"

"Nothing released this morning."

"Have they reached any conclusions abut the vandalism?"

"Not that I've heard."

"Well, I observed something last night that looks interesting. All four items that were damaged were portrayals of the female figure, more or less unclothed. Did the police notice that?"

"I don't know," said the police reporter. "I'll mention it at Headquarters."

"It isn't easy to spot. The stuff is pretty abstract, and a casual glance wouldn't tell anything."

"Then the vandal must have been someone who digs modern art," said Kendall. "Some kind of nut who hated his mother."

"That narrows it down," said Arch.

Qwilleran was in his element—on the fringe of the police beat where he had learned the newspaper craft. His face had a glow. Even his moustache looked happy.

Three corned beef sandwiches came to the table with a plastic squeeze bottle, and the newsmen concentrated on applying mustard, each in his fashion: Arch squirting it on the rye bread in concentric circles, Kendall limning a precise zigzag, and Qwilleran squeezing out a reckless abstraction.

After a while Kendall said to him, "Know much about Lambreth?"

"I just met him once. He was sort of a stuffed shirt."

"Was the gallery successful?"

"Hard to say. It was sumptuously furnished, but that doesn't prove anything. Some of the paintings were priced in five figures, although I wouldn't give you five cents for them. I imagine investors were buying this kind of art; that's why Lambreth set up shop in the financial district."

"Maybe some sucker thought he'd been taken and got into a fatal argument with the dealer."

"That doesn't fit in with the nature of the vandalism."

Arch said, "Do you think the choice of weapon indicates anything?"

"It was a chisel from the workbench," said Kendall.

"Either the killer seized on that in a moment of passion, or he knew in advance it would be there for the purpose."

"Who was employed in the workroom?"

"I don't think anyone was employed," said Qwilleran. "I suspect Lambreth made the frames himself—in spite of the fancy front he put on for customers. When I was there, I noticed definite evidence of work in progress—but no workman. And when I asked who made the frames, he gave me an evasive answer. Then I noticed that his hands were grimy—you know, stained and battered as if he did manual labor."

"Then maybe the gallery wasn't too successful, and he was cutting corners."

"On the other hand, he was living in a good neighborhood, and his house appeared to be furnished expensively."

Kendall said, "I wonder if Lambreth admitted the killer to the premises after hours. Or did the killer let himself in the back way—with a key?"

"I'm sure it was someone Lambreth knew," Qwilleran said, "and I think the evidence of a struggle was rigged after the murder."

"How do you figure that?"

"From the position of the body. Lambreth seemed to have gone down between his swivel chair and his desk, as if he had been sitting there when the murderer took him by surprise. He wouldn't engage in a brawl and then go and sit at his desk, waiting to be polished off."

"Well, let the police solve it," said Arch. "We've got work to do."

As the men left the lunch table, the bartender beckoned to Qwilleran. "I read about the Lambreth murder," he said and paused significantly before adding, "I know that gallery."

"You do? What do you know about it?"

"Lambreth was a crook."

"What makes you think so?"

Bruno gave a hasty glance up and down the bar. "I know a lot of painters and sculptors, and any one of them can tell you how Lambreth operated. He'd sell something for $800 and give the artist a measly $150."

"You think one of your pals wiped him out?"

Bruno was suitably indignant. "I wasn't saying anything like that. I just thought you'd like to know what kind of a guy he was."

"Well, thanks."

"And his wife isn't much better."

"What do you mean by that?"

The bartender picked up a towel and wiped the bar where it didn't need wiping. "Everybody knows she's been playing around. You've got to hand it to her, though. She tiddley-winks where it'll do the most good."

"Like where?"

"Like upstairs over where you live. I understand it's quite a cozy apartment up there." Bruno stopped wiping the bar and gave Qwilleran a significant look. "She goes up there to paint the cat!"

Qwilleran shrugged a no comment and started to leave.

Bruno called him back. "Something else, too, Mr. Qwilleran," he said. "I heard about some funny business at the museum. There's a valuable art object missing, and they're hushing it up."

"Why would they hush it up?"

"Who knows? A lot of funny things go on at that place."

"What's missing?"

"A dagger—from the Florentine Room! This friend of mine—he's a guard at the museum—he discovered the dagger was missing and reported it, but nobody wants to do anything about it. I thought it might be a scoop for you."

"Thanks. I'll look into it," said Qwilleran. Some of his best tips had come from Press Club bartenders. Also some of the worst.

On the way out of the building he stopped in the lobby where the ladies of the press were running a benefit sale of secondhand books. For a half-dollar he picked up a copy of *Keeping Your Pet Happy*. He also bought A *Study of Crests and Troughs in American Business from 1800 to 1850* for a dime.

Back at the office he telephoned the Lambreth home. Butchy answered and said no, Zoe couldn't come to the phone . . . yes, she had managed to get some sleep . . . no, there was nothing Qwilleran could do.

He finished his afternoon's work and went home with his coat collar turned up against the snow that had started to fall. He thought he would feed the cat, go out and grab a hamburger somewhere, and then wander over to the art museum to look at the Florentine Room. It was Thursday, and the museum was open late.

When he arrived at No. 26, shaking the snow from his shoulders and stamping his feet, he found Koko waiting for him. The cat greeted him in the front hall—not with a noisy bill of complaints this time but an appreciative squeak. The way his whiskers tilted upward gave him a pleasant look of expectancy. The newsman felt flattered.

"Hello, old fellow," he said. "Did you have an eventful day?"

From Koko's noncommittal murmur, Qwilleran decided the cat's day had been somewhat less interesting than his own. He started upstairs to carve the tenderloin—or whatever one called the cut of beef that Mountclemens supplied for catfood—and noted that Koko did not bound ahead of him. Instead the cat was dogging his heels and getting between his ankles as he climbed the stairs.

"What are you trying to do? Trip me?" Qwilleran said.

He prepared the beef according to official instructions, placed the dish on the floor, and sat down to watch Koko eat. He was beginning to appreciate the fine points of Siamese design—the elegant proportions of the body, the undulating muscles beneath the fine coat, and the exquisite shading of the fur from off-white to pale fawn to the darkest of velvety browns. Qwilleran decided it was the finest shade of brown he had ever seen.

To his surprise, the cat showed no interest in food. He wanted to rub ankles and utter plaintive high-pitched mews.

"What's the matter with you?" said Qwilleran. "You're a hard one to figure out."

The cat looked up with a beseeching expression in his blue eyes, purred loudly and raised one paw to Qwilleran's knee.

"Koko, I'll bet you're lonesome. You're used to having someone around all day. Are you feeling neglected?"

He lifted the willing bundle of warm fur to his shoulder, and Koko purred in his ear with a rasping undertone that denoted extreme satisfaction.

"I think I'll stay home tonight," Qwilleran told the cat. "Weather's bad. Snow's getting deep. Left my rubbers at the office."

Scrounging for something to eat, he helped himself to a slice of Koko's *pâté de la maison*. It was the best meat loaf he had ever tasted. Koko sensed that this was a party and began to race from one end of the apartment to the other. He seemed to be flying low over the carpet, his feet moving but never touching the floor—up over the desk in a single leap, then from chair to bookshelf to table to another chair to cabinet top—all with bewildering speed. Qwilleran began to realize why there were no table lamps in the apartment.

He too wandered around—at a more leisurely rate. He opened a door in the long narrow hall and found a bedroom with a four-poster bed that had red velvet side curtains and a canopy. In the bathroom he found a green flask labeled *Essence of Lime*; he took a sniff and recognized the scent. In the living room he strolled with his hands in his pants pockets, enjoying a close inspection of Mountclemens' treasures; engraved brass labels on the picture frames said *Hals*, *Gauguin*, *Eakins*.

So this was a love nest, according to Bruno. Qwilleran had to agree it was well equipped for the purpose: dim lights, soft music, candles, wine, big loungy chairs—everything to induce a mellow mood.

And now Earl Lambreth was dead! Qwilleran blew through his moustache as he considered the possibilities. It was not difficult to visualize Mountclemens as a wife-stealer. The critic had a suave charm that would appeal to any woman he chose to impress—and an authority that would never take no for an answer. Wife-stealer, yes. Murderer, no. Mountclemens was too elegant, too fastidious for that.

Eventually Qwilleran returned to his own apartment, followed by a genial Koko. For the cat's amusement, Qwilleran tied a wad of folded paper to a length of string and dangled it. At nine o'clock the final edition of the *Daily Fluxion* was delivered, and Koko perused the headlines. When the newsman finally settled down in an easy chair with a book, the cat took possession of his lap, the silky fur testifying to a state of contentment. It was with apparent reluctance that Koko took leave at midnight and went upstairs to his cushion on top of the refrigerator.

Qwilleran described his evening of cat-sitting the next day when he stopped at Arch Riker's desk to pick up his paycheck.

Arch said, "How are you hitting it off with the critic's cat?"

"Koko was lonesome last night, so I stayed home and entertained him. We played Sparrow."

"Is this some parlor game I'm not familiar with?"

"It's something we invented—like tennis, with one player

and no net," said Qwilleran. "I make a sparrow out of paper and tie it to a piece of string. Then I swing it back and forth while Koko bats it with his paw. He's got a substantial backhand, I want you to know. Every time he connects, he gets one point. If he strikes and misses, that's a point for me. Twenty-one points is game. I'm keeping a running score. After five games last night it was Koko 108 and Qwilleran 92."

"I'm betting on the cat all the way," said Arch. He reached for a sheet of pink paper. "I know that cat consumes a lot of your time, attention and physical strength, but I wish you'd give me some action on that Halapay profile. Another pink memo came up this morning."

"I'll be all set as soon as I have one more meeting with Mrs. Halapay," said Qwilleran.

Returning to his desk, he called Sandy and suggested lunch the following Wednesday.

"Let's make it for dinner," she suggested. "Cal is in Denmark, and I'm all alone. I'd love to go to dinner where there's a dance band. You're such a wonderful dancer." Her laughter left the sincerity of her compliment in doubt.

*Be Nice to People,* said the slogan on his telephone, and he replied, "Sandy, I'd enjoy that very much—but not next week. I'll be working nights." The telephone said nothing about lying to people. "Let's just have lunch on Wednesday and discuss your husband's charities and civic activities. They've given me a firm deadline on this profile."

"All right," she said. "I'll pick you up, and we'll drive out somewhere. We'll have scads to talk about. I want to hear all about the Lambreth murder."

"I'm afraid I don't know much about it."

"Why, I think it's all perfectly obvious."

"What's obvious?"

"That it's a family affair." Weighted pause. "You know what was going on, don't you?"

"No, I don't."

"Well, I wouldn't want to discuss it on the phone," she said. "See you Wednesday at noon."

Qwilleran spent the morning finishing up odds and ends. He wrote a short humorous piece about a local graphics artist who had switched to watercolors after dropping a hundred-pound lithograph stone on his foot. Then he did an inspirational story about a prizewinning textile weaver who was also a high-school math teacher, author of two published novels, licensed pilot, cellist, and mother of ten. Next he considered the talented poodle who paw-painted pictures. The poodle was having a show at the humane society shelter.

Just as Qwilleran was visualizing the headline (*One-Dog Exhibition of Poodle Doodles*), the telephone on his desk rang. He answered, and a low, breathy voice gave him a ripple of pleasure.

"This is Zoe Lambreth, Mr. Qwilleran. I must speak softly. Can you hear me?"

"Yes. Is anything wrong?"

"I need to talk with you—in person—if you can spare the time. Not here. Downtown."

"Would the Press Club be all right?"

"Is there some place more private? I'd like to talk confidentially."

"Would you mind coming to my apartment?"

"That would be better. You live in Mountclemens' building, don't you?"

"No. 26 Blenheim Place."

"I know where it is."

"How about tomorrow afternoon? Take a taxi. It isn't a nice neighborhood."

"Tomorrow. Thank you so much. I need your advice. I must hang up now."

There was an abrupt click, and the voice was gone. Qwilleran's moustache virtually danced. *Widow of Slain Art Dealer Reveals Story to Flux Reporter.*

## CHAPTER NINE

It had been a long time since Qwilleran had entertained a woman in his apartment, and he waked Saturday morning with a mild case of stage fright. He swallowed a cup of instant coffee, gnawed on a stale doughnut, and wondered if he should serve Zoe something to eat or drink. Coffee seemed suitable under the circumstances. Coffee and what? Doughnuts would look frivolous; why, he couldn't explain. Cake? Too pretentious. Cookies?

There was a grocery in the neighborhood that specialized in beer, cheap wine and gummy white bread. Dubiously Qwilleran inspected their packaged cookies, but the ingredients listed in small type (artificial flavoring, emulsifier, glycerine, lecithin and invert syrup) dampened his interest.

He inquired for a bakery and walked six blocks through February slush to a shop where the merchandise appeared edible. Vetoing *petit fours* (too fancy) and oatmeal cookies (too hearty), he settled on chocolate chip cookies and bought two pounds.

There was an old-fashioned percolator in his kitchenette, but how it operated was a mystery to him. Zoe would have to accept instant coffee. He wondered if she used sugar and cream. Back he went to the grocery store for a pound of sugar, a half pint of coffee cream and some paper napkins.

By that time it was noon, and a reluctant February sun began slanting into the apartment, exposing dust on the tables, lint on the rug, and cat hair on the sofa. Qwilleran dusted with paper napkins, then hurried upstairs to Mountclemens' apartment to hunt for a vacuum cleaner. He found one in a broom closet in the kitchen.

One o'clock came, and he was ready—except for cigarettes. He had forgotten cigarettes. He rushed out to the drugstore and bought something long, mild and unfiltered. After debating about the filter, he decided Zoe was not one to compromise.

At one-thirty he lighted the gas logs in the fireplace and sat down to wait.

Zoe arrived promptly at four. Qwilleran saw a lovely woman in a soft brown fur coat step from a taxi, look up and down the street, and hurry up to the portico. He was there to meet her.

"Thank you so much for letting me come," she said in a low-pitched, breathless voice. "Butchy has been watching me like a hawk, and I had to sneak out of the house. . . . I shouldn't complain. At a time like this you need a friend like Butchy." She dropped her brown alligator handbag. "I'm sorry. I'm very much upset."

"Just take it easy," said Qwilleran, "and gather yourself together. Would a cup of coffee feel good?"

"I'd better not have coffee," she said. "It makes me nervous, and I'm jumpy enough as it is." She gave Qwilleran her coat and took a seat in a straight-backed pull-up chair, crossing her knees attractively. "Do you mind if we close the door?"

"Not at all, although there's no one else in the house."

"I had an uneasy feeling I was being followed. I took a cab

to the Arcade Building, then walked through and picked up another one at the other entrance. Do you think they might have someone following me? The police, I mean."

"I don't see why they should. What gave you that idea?"

"They came to the house yesterday. Two of them. Two detectives. They were perfect gentlemen, but some of their questions were upsetting, as if they were trying to trap me. Do you suppose they suspect *me?*"

"Not really, but they have to cover every possibility."

"Butchy was there, of course, and she was quite antagonistic toward the detectives. It didn't look good at all. She's so protective, you know. Altogether it was a terrible experience."

"What did they say when they left?"

"They thanked me for my cooperation and said they might want to talk to me again. After that I telephoned you—while Butchy was down in the basement. I didn't want her to know."

"Why not?"

"Well . . . because she's so sure she can handle everything herself in this—this crisis. And also because of what I'm going to tell you. . . . You don't suppose the police would be watching my movements, do you? Maybe I shouldn't have come here."

"Why shouldn't you come here, Mrs. Lambreth? I'm a friend of the family. I'm professionally connected with the art field. And I'm going to help you with details concerning the gallery. How does that sound?"

She smiled bleakly. "I'm beginning to feel like a criminal. One has to be so careful in talking to the police. If you use the wrong word or put the wrong inflection in your voice, they pounce on it."

"Well, now," said Qwilleran in his most soothing way, "put that episode out of your mind and relax. Wouldn't you like a more comfortable chair?"

"This is fine. I have a better command of myself when I sit up straight."

She was wearing a pale blue dress of fuzzy wool that made her look soft and fragile. Qwilleran tried not to stare at the provocative indentation just below her kneecap.

He said, "I find this a very comfortable apartment. My landlord has a knack for furnishing a place. How did you know I was staying here?"

"Oh . . . things get around in art circles."

"Apparently you've been to this house before."

"Mountclemens had us to dinner once or twice."

"You must know him better than most artists do."

"We've been fairly friendly. I did several studies of his cat. Did you notify him—about the—?"

"I haven't been able to find out where he stays in New York. Do you know his hotel?"

"It's near the Museum of Modern Art, but I can't remember the name." She was twisting the handle of her handbag that lay on her lap.

Qwilleran brought a plate from the kitchenette. "Would you care for some cookies?"

"No, thanks. I have to—count—calories—" Her voice trailed away.

He sensed her preoccupation and said, "Now what is it that you want to tell me?" With the other half of his mind he was taking Zoe's measurements and wondering why she worried about calories.

"I don't know how to begin."

"How about a cigarette? I'm forgetting my manners."

"I gave them up a few months ago."

"Mind if I light my pipe?"

Abruptly Zoe said, "I didn't tell the police everything."

"No?"

"It may have been wrong, but I couldn't bring myself to answer some of their questions."

"What kind of questions?"

"They asked if Earl had any enemies. How could I point a finger at someone and say he was an enemy? What would happen if I started naming people all over the city? Acquaintances . . . fellow club members . . . important people. I think that was a terrible thing to ask, don't you?"

"It was a necessary question. In fact," said Qwilleran, in a kind but firm way, "I'm going to ask you the same question. Did he have many enemies?"

"I'm afraid so. A lot of people disliked him. . . . Mr. Qwilleran, it's all right to talk confidentially to you, isn't it? I must confide in someone. I'm sure you're not one of those sneaky reporters who would—"

"Those characters are only in the movies," he assured her. His attitude was all sympathy and interest.

Zoe sighed heavily and began. "There's a lot of competition and jealousy in the art field. I don't know why it should be."

"That's true in all fields."

"It's worse among artists. Believe me!"

"Could you be more specific?"

"Well . . . the gallery directors, for example. The other galleries in town felt that Earl was luring their best artists away from them."

"Was he?"

Zoe bristled slightly. "Naturally, the artists wanted to be represented by the foremost gallery. As a result, Earl showed better work, and the Lambreth exhibitions got better reviews."

"And the jealousy increased."

Zoe nodded. "Besides, Earl often had to reject the work of second-rate artists, and that didn't win him any friends! It made him a villain. An artist's ego is a precious thing. People like Cal Halapay and Franz Buchwalter—or Mrs. Buchwalter, to be exact—did a lot of talking about my husband at the club, and it wasn't nice. That's why Earl would never go to the Turp and Chisel."

"So far," said Qwilleran, "you've mentioned only outsiders who were unfriendly. Was there anyone within the organization who didn't get along with your husband?"

Zoe hesitated. She looked apologetic. "Nobody really warmed up to him. He had an aloof manner. It was only a facade, but few people understood that."

"There's the possibility that the crime was committed by someone who had a key to the gallery or was willingly admitted to the premises."

"That's what Butchy said."

"Did anyone but you have a key?"

"N-no," said Zoe, groping in the depths of her handbag.

Qwilleran said, "Can I get you something?"

"Maybe I'll have a glass of water—with some ice. It's rather warm—"

He turned down the flame in the fireplace and brought Zoe a drink of ice water. "Tell me about your friend Butchy. I understand she's a sculptor."

"Yes. Welded metal," Zoe said in a bleak voice.

"You mean she uses a torch and all that? It might make a story. Lady welders are always good for some space—with a photograph of sparks flying."

Zoe nodded slowly as she considered the idea. "Yes, I wish you would write something about Butchy. It would do her a lot of good—psychologically. Not long ago she lost a $50,000 commission, and it was a damaging setback. You see, she teaches at Penniman School, and the commission would have enhanced her prestige."

"How did she lose out?"

"Butchy was being considered to do the outdoor sculpture

for a new shopping center. Then suddenly the commission was awarded to Ben Riggs, who shows at the Lambreth Gallery."

"Was the switch justified?"

"Oh, yes. Riggs is a much better artist. He works in clay and casts in bronze. But it was a blow to Butchy. I'd like to do something to help her. Would you write her up for the paper?"

"She's a good friend of yours?" Qwilleran was comparing the soft, attractive Zoe with the mannish character who had been guarding her on the night of the murder.

"Yes and no. We grew up together and went to art school at the same time, and Butchy was my best friend when we were both at the tomboy age. But Butchy never outgrew that stage. She was always big and husky for a girl, and she bluffed it off by acting boyish. I feel sorry for Butchy. We don't have much in common anymore—except old times."

"How did she happen to be at your house Wednesday night?"

"She was the only one I could think to call. After finding Earl and notifying the police, I was in a daze. I didn't know what to do. I needed someone, and so I called Butchy. She came right away and drove me home and said she'd stay with me for a few days. Now I can't get rid of her."

"How come?"

"She enjoys being my protector. She needs to feel needed. Butchy doesn't have many friends, and she has an annoying way of clutching at the few she has."

"What did your husband think of her?"

"He didn't like her at all. Earl wanted me to drop Butchy, but it's hard to break off with someone you've known all your life—especially when your paths are crossing all the time. . . . I don't know why I'm telling you these personal details. I must be boring you."

110

"Not at all. You're—"

"I needed to talk to someone who's disinterested and sympathetic. You're very easy to talk to. Is that typical of newspapermen?"

"We're good listeners."

"I feel much better now, thanks to you." Zoe leaned back in her chair and was silent, and a tenderness crept into her face.

Qwilleran smoothed his moustache with the stem of his pipe and beamed inwardly. He said, "I'm glad I could—"

"Are you looking for material for your column?" Zoe interrupted, the radiance of her expression seeming inappropriate for the question.

"Of course, I'm always—"

"I'd like to tell you about Nino." She pronounced the name "Nine-oh."

"Who's Nino?" said Qwilleran, camouflaging a mild disappointment with a brisk tone.

"He's a Thingist. Some people call him a junk sculptor. He makes meaningful constructions out of junk and calls them Things."

"I saw them at the gallery. One was a piece of sewer pipe stuck with bicycle spokes."

Zoe gave him a luminous smile. "That's 'Thing #17.' Isn't it eloquent? It affirms life while repudiating the pseudo-world around us. Weren't you gripped by its rebellious tensions?"

"To tell you the truth . . . no," said Qwilleran, a trifle peevishly. "It looked like a piece of sewer pipe and some bicycle spokes."

Zoe gave him a sweet look in which reproach mingled with pity. "Your eye isn't tuned to contemporary expression as yet, but you'll develop appreciation in time."

Qwilleran squirmed and scowled down at his moustache.

Enthusiastically Zoe went on. "Nino is my protégé, more or less. I discovered him. This city has some talented artists, but I can honestly say that Nino has more than talent. He has genius. You should visit his studio." She leaned forward eagerly. "Would you like to meet Nino? I'm sure he'd make good material for a story."

"What's his full name?"

"Nine Oh Two Four Six Eight Three," she said. "Or maybe it's Five. I can never remember the last digit. We call him Nino for short."

"You mean he has a number instead of a name?"

"Nino is a disaffiliate," she explained. "He doesn't subscribe to the conventions of ordinary society."

"He wears a beard, of course."

"Yes, he does. How did you know? He even speaks a language of his own, but we don't expect conformity of a genius, do we? Using a number instead of a name is part of his Protest. I think only his mother and the Social Security people know his real name."

Qwilleran stared at her. "Where does this character hang out?"

"He lives and works in an alley garage at Twelfth and Somers, behind an iron foundry. His studio may shock you."

"I don't think I shock easily."

"I mean you may be disturbed by his collection of Found Objects."

"Junk?"

"It isn't all junk. He has a few very fine things. Heaven knows where he gets them. But mostly it's junk—beautiful junk. Nino's talent for alley-picking amounts to a divine gift. If you go to see him, try to understand the nature of his artistic vision. He sees beauty where others see only trash and filth."

Qwilleran studied Zoe with fascination—her quiet animation, her obvious conviction. He didn't understand what she was talking about, but he enjoyed being under her spell.

"I think you'll like Nino," she went on. "He is elemental and real—and sad, in a way. Or perhaps you and I are the sad ones, conducting ourselves according to a prescribed pattern. It's like following the steps of a dance composed by a dictatorial dancing master. The dance of life should be created from moment to moment with individuality and spontaneity."

Qwilleran roused himself from a rapt stare and said, "May I ask you a personal question? Why do you paint such incomprehensible things when you have the ability to make real pictures of real things?"

Zoe gazed at him sweetly again. "You are so naïve, Mr. Qwilleran, but you are honest, and that is refreshing. Real pictures of real things can be done by a camera. I paint in the exploratory spirit of today. We don't have all the answers, and we know it. Sometimes I'm bewildered by my own creations, but they are my artistic response to life as I see it today. True art is always an expression of its time."

"I see." He wanted to be convinced, but he wasn't sure that Zoe had succeeded.

"Someday we must discuss this subject at great length." There was an unaccountable yearning in her expression.

"I'd enjoy that," he said softly.

A self-conscious silence loomed between them. Qwilleran breached it by offering her a cigarette.

"I've given them up," she reminded him.

"Cookie? They're chocolate chip."

"No, thanks." She sighed.

He pointed to the Monet over the fireplace. "What do you think of that? It came with the apartment."

"If it were a good one, Mountclemens wouldn't squander it

on a tenant," she said with an abrupt edge to her voice, and her quick change of mood astonished Qwilleran.

"But it has a nice frame," he said. "Who makes the frames at the Lambreth Gallery?"

"Why do you ask?"

"Just curious. People have remarked about their fine workmanship." It was a lie but the kind of lie that always elicited confidences.

"Oh . . . Well, I might as well tell you. It was Earl. He made all the frames himself, although he never wanted it known. It would have destroyed the prestige image of the gallery."

"He was a hard worker—making frames, keeping the books, tending shop."

"Yes. The last time I saw him alive he was complaining about the work load."

"Why didn't he hire help?"

Zoe shrugged and shook her head.

It was an unsatisfactory answer, but Qwilleran let it pass. He said, "Have you remembered anything that might help the investigation? Anything your husband said when you were there at five-thirty?"

"Nothing of any importance. Earl showed me some graphics that had just come in, and I told him—" She stopped abruptly. "Yes, there was a phone call—"

"Anything unusual about that?"

"I wasn't listening particularly, but there was something Earl said—now that I remember it—that doesn't make sense. It was about the station wagon."

"Did your husband have a wagon?"

"Every dealer has to have one. I hate them."

"What did he say about the wagon?"

"I wasn't paying too much attention, but I heard something about putting paintings in the station wagon for delivery. Earl said the wagon was in the alley; in fact, he repeated it rather emphatically. That's why it comes to mind. . . . I didn't think of it at the time, but now it seems strange."

"Why does it strike you as strange?"

"Our car was at the repair shop, having a tune-up. It's still there. I never picked it up. Earl had dropped it off at the garage that morning. And yet he was insisting—on the telephone—that it was in the alley, as if the other party was giving him an argument."

"Do you know who was on the line?" Qwilleran asked.

"No. It sounded like long distance. You know how people shout when it's long distance. Even when it's a perfectly good connection they think they have to pitch their voices higher."

"Maybe your husband was telling a little white lie—for business reasons."

"I don't know."

"Or maybe he was referring to some other dealer's station wagon."

"I really don't know."

"You didn't see anything parked in the alley?"

"No. I went in the front door and left the same way. And when I went back at seven o'clock, there was no car of any kind in the alley. Do you think the phone call has any bearing on what happened?"

"It wouldn't hurt to tell the police about it. Try to remember as much as you can."

Zoe lapsed into a reverie.

"By the way," Qwilleran said, "does Mountclemens have a car?"

"No," she murmured.

Qwilleran took a long time to refill his pipe, tapping it noisily on the ashtray. As if in answer to his signal, there was a prolonged, desolate wail outside the apartment door.

"That's Koko," said Qwilleran. "He objects to being excluded. Mind if he comes in?"

"Oh, I adore Kao K'o-Kung!"

Qwilleran opened the door, and the cat—after his usual reconnaissance—walked in, his tail moving from side to side in graceful arabesques. He had been sleeping and had not yet limbered his muscles. Now he arched his back in a taut curve, after which he extended two forward legs in a luxurious stretch. He concluded by making a long leg to the rear.

Zoe said, "He limbers up like a dancer."

"You want to see him dance?" said Qwilleran. He folded a piece of paper and tied it to a string. In anticipation Koko took a few small steps to the left and a few to the right, then rose on his hind feet as the bauble started to swing. He was all grace and rhythm, dancing on his *pointes*, leaping, executing incredible acrobatic feats in midair, landing lightly, and leaping again, higher than before.

Zoe said, "I've never seen him perform like that. Such elevation! He's a real Nijinsky."

"Mountclemens stresses intellectual pursuits," Qwilleran said, "and this cat has spent too much time on the bookshelves. I hope to broaden his range of interests. He needs more athletics."

"I'd like to make some sketches." She dived into her handbag. "He does a *grand battement* just like a ballet dancer."

A ballet dancer. *A ballet dancer.* The words brought a picture to Qwilleran's mind: a cluttered office, a painting hung crookedly on the wall. The second time he had seen that office, over a patrolman's shoulder, there was a body on the floor. And where was the painting? Qwilleran could not remember seeing the ballet dancer.

He said to Zoe, "There was a painting of a ballet dancer at the Lambreth Gallery—"

"Earl's famous Ghirotto," she said, as she sketched rapidly on a pad. "It was only half of the original canvas, you know. It was his one great ambition to find the other half. It would have made him rich, he thought."

Qwilleran was alerted. "How rich?"

"If the two halves were joined and properly restored, the painting would probably be worth $150,000."

The newsman blew astonishment through his moustache.

"There's a monkey on the other half," she said. "Ghirotto painted ballerinas or monkeys during his celebrated Vibrato Period, but only once did he paint both dancer and monkey in the same composition. It was a unique piece—a collector's dream. After the war it was shipped to a New York dealer and damaged in transit—ripped down the middle. Because of the way the picture was composed, the importer was able to frame the two halves and sell them separately. Earl bought the half with the dancer and hoped to trace the half with the monkey."

Qwilleran said, "Do you suppose the owner of the monkey has been trying to trace the ballet dancer?"

"Could be. Earl's half is the valuable one; it has the artist's signature." As she talked, her pencil skimmed over the paper, and her glance darted between sketch pad and performing cat.

"Did many people know about the Ghirotto?"

"Oh, it was quite a conversation piece. Several people wanted to buy the ballerina—just on speculation. Earl could have sold it and made a nice little profit, but he was holding out for his dream of $150,000. He never gave up hope of finding the monkey."

Qwilleran proceeded circumspectly. "Did you see the ballerina on the night of the crime?"

Zoe laid down her pencil and pad. "I'm afraid I didn't see much of anything—that night."

"I was there, snooping around," Qwilleran said, "and I'm pretty sure the painting was gone."

"Gone!"

"It had been hanging over the desk on my previous visit, and now I remember—the night the police were there—that wall was vacant."

"What should I do?"

"Better tell the police. It looks as if the painting's been stolen. Tell them about the phone call, too. When you get home, call the Homicide Bureau. Do you remember the detectives names? Hames and Wojcik."

Zoe clapped both hands to her face in dismay. "Honestly, I had forgotten all about that Ghirotto!"

# CHAPTER TEN

When Zoe had gone from Qwilleran's apartment—leaving him with a can of coffee, a pound of sugar, a half-pint of cream, a pack of cigarettes, and two pounds of chocolate chip cookies—he wondered how much information she had withheld. Her nervousness suggested she was sifting the facts. She had stammered when asked if anyone else had a key to the Lambreth Gallery. Admittedly she had avoided telling the police everything that occurred to her. And she claimed to have forgotten the existence of a painting valuable enough—possibly—to make murder worthwhile.

Qwilleran went upstairs to prepare Koko's dinner. Slowly and absently he diced meat while pondering other complications in the Lambreth case. How valid was Sandy's hint that this was "a family affair"? And how would that connect with the disappearance of the Ghirotto? There was also the vandalism to take into account, and Qwilleran reflected that the missing painting fell in the same category as the damaged subjects; it depicted the female figure in skimpy attire.

He opened the kitchen door and looked out. The night was crisp, and the neighborhood smells were made more pungent by the cold. Carbon monoxide hung in the air, and oily rags had been burned at the corner garage. Down below him was the patio, a dark hole, its high brick walls cutting off any light from distant streetlamps.

Qwilleran turned on the exterior light, which cast a weak yellow glow on the fire escape, and thought, What does that guy have against using a little extra electricity? He remembered seeing a flashlight in the broom closet, and he went to get it—an efficient, long-handled, well-balanced, powerful, chrome-plated beauty. Everything Mountclemens owned was well-designed: knives, pots and pans, even the flashlight. It threw a strong beam on the walls and floor of the empty patio, on the ponderous wooden gate, on the wooden fire escape. Patches of frozen slush clung to the steps, and Qwilleran decided to postpone further investigation until daylight. Tomorrow he might even take Koko down there for a romp.

That evening he went to dinner at a nearby Italian restaurant, and the brown-eyed waitress reminded him of Zoe. He went home and played Sparrow with Koko, and the cat's movements reminded him of the missing ballet dancer. He lighted the gas logs in the fireplace and scanned the second-hand book on economics that he had bought at the Press Club; the statistics reminded him of Nine Oh Two Four Six Eight Three—or was it Five?

On Sunday he went to visit Nino.

The artist's studio-home in an alley garage was as dismal as it sounded. A former occupant had left the building coated with grease, to which was added the blight of Nino's collection of junk.

Having knocked and received no answer, Qwilleran walked into the agglomeration of joyless castoffs. There were old tires, bushels of broken glass, chunks of uprooted concrete sidewalk, tin cans of every size, and dispossessed doors and windows. He made note of a baby carriage without wheels, a store window mannequin with arms and head missing, a kitchen sink painted bright orange inside and out, an iron gate covered with rust, and a wooden bedstead in the depressing modernistic design of the 1930's.

A heater suspended from the ceiling belched warm fumes in Qwilleran's face, while the cold drafts at ankle level were paralyzing. Also suspended from the ceiling by a rope was a crystal chandelier of incredible beauty.

Then Qwilleran saw the artist at work. On a platform at the rear stood a monstrous Thing made of wooden oddments, ostrich plumes and bits of shiny tin. Nino was affixing two baby carriage wheels to the monster's head.

He gave the wheels a twirl and stood back, and the spinning spokes, glinting under a spotlight, became malevolent eyes.

"Good afternoon," said Qwilleran. "I'm a friend of Zoe Lambreth. You must be Nino."

The sculptor appeared to be in a trance, his face illumined with the thrill of creation. His shirt and trousers were stiff with paint and grease, his beard needed trimming, and his hair had not recently known a comb. In spite of it all, he was a good-looking brute—with classic features and an enviable physique. He looked at Qwilleran without seeing him, then admiringly he turned back to the Thing with spinning eyes.

"Have you given it a title?" asked the newsman.

" 'Thirty-six,' " said Nino, and he put his face in his hands and cried. Qwilleran waited sympathetically until the artist had recovered and then said, "How do you create these works of art? What is your procedure?"

"I live them," said Nino. "Thirty-six is what I am, I was and I will be. Yesterday is gone, and who cares? If I set fire to this studio, I live—in every leaping flame, flash, flare, floriferous flourish."

"Do you have your materials insured?"

"If I do, I do. If I don't, I don't. It's all relative. Man loves, hates, cries, plays, but what can an artist do? BOOM! That's the way it goes. A world beyond a world beyond a world beyond a world."

"A cosmic concept," Qwilleran agreed, "but do people really understand your ideas?"

"They wear out their brains trying, but I know, and you know, and we all know—what do we know? Nothing!"

Nino was edging closer to the newsman in his enthusiasm for this conversation, and Qwilleran backed away discreetly. He said, "Nino, you appear to be a pessimist, but doesn't your success at the Lambreth Gallery help to give you an affirmative attitude toward life?"

"Warm, wanton, wary, weak woman! I talk to her. She talks to me. We communicate."

"Did you know her husband is dead? Murdered!"

"We are all dead," said Nino. "Dead as doorknobs . . . *Doorknobs!*" he shouted and plunged into a mountain of junk in desperate search.

"Thank you for letting me see your studio," said Qwilleran, and he started toward the door. As he passed a littered shelf, a gleam of gold signaled to him, and he called back over his shoulder, "Here's a doorknob, if that's what you're hunting for."

There were two doorknobs on the shelf, and they looked like pure gold. With them were other pieces of bright metal, as well as some startling pieces of carved ivory and jade, but Qwilleran did not stop to examine them. The fumes from the heater had made his head throb, and he was making a dash for the fresh air. He wanted to go home and spend a sane, sensible, sanitary Sunday with Koko. He was becoming attached to that cat, he told himself, and he would be sorry when Mountclemens returned. He wondered if Koko really liked the cultural climate upstairs. Were the pleasures of reading headlines and sniffing old masters preferable to an exhilarating game of Sparrow? After four days of play, the score was 471 for the cat, 409 for the man.

When Qwilleran arrived home, anticipating a friendly, furry, frolicsome fuss at the door, he was disappointed. Koko was not waiting for him. He went upstairs to Mountclemens' apartment and found the door closed. He heard music within. He knocked.

There was a delay before Mountclemens, wearing a dressing gown, answered the knock.

"I see you're home," said Qwilleran. "Just wanted to be sure the cat was getting his supper."

"He has finished the entrée," said Mountclemens, "and is now relishing a poached egg yolk as a savory. Thank you for taking care of him. He looks well and happy."

"We had some good times together," said Qwilleran. "We played games."

"Indeed! I have often wished he would learn mah-jongg."

"Did you hear the bad news about the Lambreth Gallery?"

"If they had a fire, they deserve it," said the critic. "That loft building is a tinderbox."

"Not a fire. A murder."

"Indeed!"

"Earl Lambreth," said Qwilleran. "His wife found him dead in his office last Wednesday night. He had been stabbed."

"How untidy!" Mountclemens' voice sounded bored—or tired—and he stepped back as if preparing to close the door.

"The police have no suspects," Qwilleran went on. "Do you have any theories?"

Curtly Mountclemens said, "I am in the process of unpacking. And I am about to bathe. There is nothing further from my mind than the identity of Earl Lambreth's murderer." His tone terminated the conversation.

Qwilleran accepted the dismissal and went downstairs, pulling at his moustache and reflecting that Mountclemens had a talent for being obnoxious when it suited his whim.

Down the street at a third-rate restaurant he later scowled at a plate of meatballs, picked at a limp salad, and contemplated a cup of hot water in which floated a tea bag. Added to his irritation with his landlord was a nagging disappointment; Koko had not come to the door to greet him. He returned home unsatisfied and disgruntled.

Qwilleran was about to unlock the vestibule door when a scent of lime peel came through the keyhole, and he was not surprised to find Mountclemens in the entrance hall.

"Oh, there you are!" said the critic amiably. "I had just come downstairs to invite you for a cup of Lapsang Souchong and some dessert. Rather laboriously I transported home a Dobos torte from a very fine Viennese bakery in New York."

The sun broke through Qwilleran's clouds, and he followed the velvet jacket and Italian pumps upstairs.

Mountclemens poured tea and described current exhibitions in New York, while Qwilleran let rich buttery chocolate melt slowly on his tongue.

"And now let us hear the gruesome details," said the critic. "I assume they are gruesome. I heard nothing about the murder in New York, where art dealers are more or less expendable. . . . Forgive me if I sit at my desk and open mail while you talk."

Mountclemens faced a stack of large and small envelopes and wrappered publications. Placing each envelope face down on the desk, he rested his right hand on it, while his left hand wielded the paper knife and extracted the contents, most of which he dropped contemptuously in the wastebasket.

Qwilleran recounted the details of Lambreth's murder briefly, as it had appeared in the newspaper. "That's the story," he said. "Any guesses as to motive?"

"Personally," said Mountclemens, "I have never been able to appreciate murder for revenge. I find murder for personal gain infinitely more appealing. But what anyone could possibly gain by dispatching Earl Lambreth to the hereafter is beyond my comprehension."

"He had quite a few enemies, I understand."

"All art dealers and all art critics have enemies!" Mountclemens gave an envelope a particularly vicious rip. "The first one who comes to mind, in this case, is that indescribable Bolton woman."

"What did the lady welder have against Lambreth?"

"He robbed her of a $50,000 commission—or so she says."

"The outdoor sculpture for the shopping center?"

"Actually Lambreth did the innocent public a favor by convincing the architects to commission another sculptor. Welded metal is a fad. If we are fortunate, it will soon die—put to death by practitioners like the Bolton creature."

Qwilleran said, "Someone suggested I write a human-interest story about her."

"By all means, interview the woman," said Mountclemens, "if only for your own education. Wear tennis shoes. If she stages one of her insane tantrums, you may have to sprint for your life or dodge metal ingots."

"She sounds like a good murder suspect."

"She has the motive and the temperament. But she did not commit the crime, I can assure you. She would be incapable of doing anything successfully—especially murder, which requires a certain amount of finesse."

Qwilleran lingered over the last few bittersweet crumbs of torte, and then he said, "I've also been wondering about the junk sculptor they call Nino. Know anything about him?"

"Brilliant, odoriferous and harmless," said Mountclemens. "Next suspect?"

"Someone has suggested it was a family affair."

"Mrs. Lambreth has too much taste to indulge in anything as vulgar as a stabbing. A shooting, perhaps, but not a stabbing. A shooting with a dainty little cloisonné pistol—or whatever women carry in those cavernous handbags. I have always had the impression those handbags were stuffed with wet diapers. But surely there would be room to accommodate a dainty little pistol in cloisonné or tortoise shell inlaid with German silver—"

Qwilleran said, "Have you ever seen the portrait she painted of her husband? It's as lifelike as a photograph and not very complimentary."

"I thank the fates I have been spared that experience. . . . No, Mr. Qwilleran, I am afraid your murderer was no artist. The textural experience of plunging a cutting tool into flesh would be extremely repugnant to a painter. A sculptor would have a greater feeling for anatomy, but he would vent his hostilities in a manner more acceptable to society—by mauling clay, chiseling stone, or torturing metal. So you might better search for an irate customer, a desperate competitor, a psychotic art-lover, or a rejected mistress."

"All of the vandalized art depicted the female figure," said Qwilleran.

R-r-rip went the letter knife. "A nice sense of discipline," said the critic. "I begin to suspect a jealous mistress."

"Did you ever have reason to suspect Earl Lambreth of unethical business dealings?"

"My dear man," said Mountclemens, "any good art dealer has the qualifications to make an outstanding jewel thief. Earl Lambreth chose to divert his talents into more orthodox channels, but beyond that I am not in a position to say. You newspapermen are all alike. Once you get your teeth into a piece of news, you must worry it to death. . . . Another cup of tea?"

The critic poured from the silver teapot and then returned to the attack on his mail. "Here is an invitation that might interest you," he said. "Have you ever been unfortunate enough to attend a Happening?" He tossed a magenta-colored announcement card to Qwilleran.

"No. What's a Happening?"

"An evening of utter boredom, perpetrated by artists and inflicted on a public that is gullible enough to pay admission. However, the invitation will admit you without charge, and you might find it a subject for a column. You might even be mildly amused. I advise you to wear old clothes."

The Happening had a name. It was called *Heavy Heavy Hangs Over Your Head*, and it was scheduled for the following evening at the Penniman School of Fine Art. Qwilleran said he would attend.

Before the newsman left Mountclemens' apartment, Koko graced the occasion with a moment of his time. The cat appeared from behind the Oriental screen, looked at Qwilleran with a casual glance, yawned widely and left the room.

# CHAPTER ELEVEN

Monday morning Qwilleran telephoned the director of the Penniman School and asked permission to interview a member of the faculty. The director was pleased. In the man's manner Qwilleran recognized the ringing bells and flashing lights that always accompanied the anticipation of free publicity.

At one o'clock the newsman appeared at the school and was directed to the welding studio—a separate building at the rear, the ivy-covered carriage house of the former Penniman estate. Inside, the studio had a mean look. It bristled with the sharp edges and thorny points of welded metal sculpture; whether the pieces were finished or unfinished, Qwilleran could not tell. Everything seemed designed to puncture flesh and tear clothing. Around the walls were gas cylinders, lengths of rubber hose, and fire extinguishers.

Butchy Bolton, formidable in coveralls and ludicrous in her tightly waved hair, was sitting alone, eating lunch from a paper sack.

"Have a sandwich," she said with a gruffness that failed to conceal her pleasure at being interviewed for the paper. "Ham on rye." She cleared a space on an asbestos-topped workbench, pushing aside wrenches, clamps, pliers and broken bricks, and she poured Qwilleran a cup of coffee strong as tar.

He ate and drank, although he had lunched well a half hour before. He knew the advantages of chewing during an interview; casual conversation replaced formal questions and answers.

They talked about their favorite restaurants and the best way to bake a ham. From there they went to diets and exercise. That led to oxyacetylene welding. While Qwilleran ate a large red apple, Butchy put on skullcap, goggles and leather gloves and showed how to puddle a metal bar and lay an even bead.

"The first semester we're lucky if we can teach the kids not to set themselves on fire," she said.

Qwilleran said, "Why do you weld metal instead of carving wood or modeling clay?"

Butchy looked at him fiercely, and it was not clear to Qwilleran whether she was going to hit him with a welding rod or whether she was thinking of a trenchant reply. "You must have been talking to that fellow Mountclemens," she said.

"No. I'm just curious. For my own education I want to know."

Butchy kicked a workbench with one of her high-laced boots. "Off the record, it's faster and cheaper," she said. "But for the paper you can say that it's something that belongs to the twentieth century. We've discovered a new sculptor's tool. Fire!"

"I suppose it appeals mostly to men."

"Nope. Some little bitty girls take the course."

"Was Nino, the junk sculptor, one of your students?"

Butchy looked back over her shoulder as if searching for a

place to spit. "He was in my class, but I couldn't teach him anything."

"I understand he's considered somewhat of a genius."

"Some people think he's a genius. I think he's a phony. How he ever got accepted by Lambreth Gallery is hard to figure."

"Mrs. Lambreth thinks highly of his work."

Butchy exhaled loudly through her nose and said nothing.

"Did Earl Lambreth share her enthusiasm?"

"Maybe so. I don't know. Earl Lambreth was no expert. He just conned a lot of people into thinking he was an expert—if you'll pardon me for slandering the dead."

"From what I hear," said Qwilleran, "quite a few people agree with you."

"Of course they agree with me. I'm right! Earl Lambreth was a phony, like Nino. They made a great pair, trying to out-phony each other." She grinned wickedly. "Of course, everybody knows how Lambreth operated."

"How do you mean?"

"No price labels. No catalog—except on big one-man shows. It was part of the so-called prestige image. If a customer liked a piece of art, Lambreth could quote any figure the traffic would bear. And when the artist got his percentage, he had no proof of the actual selling price."

"You think there was some juggling going on?"

"Of course there was. And Lambreth got away with it because most artists are fools. Nino was the only one who accused Lambreth of rooking him. It takes a phony to know a phony."

Smugly, Butchy patted the tight waves on her head.

Qwilleran went back to the office and wrote a requisition to the Photo Department for a close-up of a lady welder at work. He also typed a rough draft of the interview—minus references to Lambreth and Nino—and put it aside to ripen. He felt pleased with himself. He felt he was on the trail of something. Next he would visit the art museum to check out the missing Florentine dagger, and after dinner he would attend the Happening. For a Monday, this was turning out to be an interesting day.

The art museum assaulted Qwilleran with its Monday afternoon quiet. In the lobby he picked up a catalog of the Florentine Collection and learned that most of it had been the generous gift of the Duxbury family. Percy Duxbury was museum commissioner. His wife was president of the fund-raising group.

At the checkroom, where Qwilleran left his hat and coat, he asked Tom LaBlanc's girl where to find the Florentine Collection.

She pointed dreamily to the far end of the corridor. "But why do you want to waste your time *there*?"

"I've never seen it, that's why. Is that a good reason?" He used an amiable, bantering tone.

She looked at him through a few strands of long hair that had fallen over one eye. "There's a loan exhibit of Swedish contemporary silver that's much more stimulating."

"Okay. I'll see both."

"You won't have time. The museum closes in an hour," she said. "The Swedish stuff is real cool, and this is the last week it will be here."

For a checkroom attendant she was taking more than routine interest in directing him, Qwilleran thought, and his professional suspicion started wigwagging to him. He went to the Florentine Room.

The Duxbury gift was a hodgepodge of paintings, tapestries, bronze reliefs, marble statues, manuscripts and small silver and gold objects in glass cases. Some were displayed behind sliding glass doors fitted with tiny, almost invisible locks; others stood on pedestals under glass domes that seemed permanently affixed.

Qwilleran ran his finger down the catalog page and found the item that interested him: a gold dagger, eight inches long, elaborately chased, sixteenth century, attributed to Benvenuto Cellini. In the glass cases—among the salt cellars and chalices and religious statues—it was not to be seen.

Qwilleran went to the director's office and asked for Mr. Farhar. A middle-aged secretary with a timid manner told him that Mr. Farhar was out. Could Mr. Smith be of assistance? Mr. Smith was chief curator.

Smith was sitting at a table covered with small jade objects, one of which he was putting under a magnifying glass. He was a handsome dark-haired man with a sallow skin and eyes that were green like the jade. Qwilleran remembered him as Humbert Humbert, Lolita's escort at the Valentine Ball. The man had a slyness in his eyes, and it was easy to suspect that he might be misbehaving in some unspeakable way. Furthermore, his first name was John; anyone called John Smith would arouse doubts in the most trusting nature.

Qwilleran said to him, "I understand there is a valuable item missing from the Florentine Room."

"Where did you hear that?"

"It was a tip that came to the paper. I don't know its source."

"The rumor is unfounded. I'm sorry you've wasted a trip. If you're looking for story material, however, you could write about this private collection of jade that has just been given to the museum by one of our commissioners."

"Thank you. I'll be glad to do that," said Qwilleran, "but at some future date. Today I'm interested in Florentine art. I'm looking particularly for a chased gold dagger attributed to Cellini, and I can't seem to find it."

Smith made a deprecating gesture. "The catalog is overly

optimistic. Very little of Cellini's work has come down to us, but the Duxburys like to think they bought a Cellini, and so we humor them."

"It's the dagger itself I want to see, regardless of who made it," said Qwilleran. "Would you be good enough to come with me and point it out?"

The curator leaned back in his chair and threw his arms up. "All right. Have it your way. The dagger is temporarily misplaced, but we don't want any publicity on it. It might touch off a wave of thefts. Such things happen, you know." He had not offered the newsman a chair.

"How much is it worth?"

"We prefer not to state."

"This is a city museum," said Qwilleran, "and the public has a right to be told about this. It might lead to its recovery. Have you notified the police?"

"If we notified the police and called the newspapers every time some small object happened to be misplaced, we would be a major nuisance."

"When did you first notice it was missing?"

Smith hesitated. "It was reported by one of the guards a week ago."

"And you've done nothing about it?"

"A routine report was placed on Mr. Farhar's desk, but—as you know—he is leaving us and has many other things on his mind."

"What time of day did the guard notice its absence?"

"In the morning when he made his first inventory check."

"How often does he check?"

"Several times a day."

"And was the dagger in the case when he made the previous check?"

"Yes."

"When was that?"

"The evening before, at closing time."

"So it disappeared during the night."

"It would seem so." John Smith was being tight-lipped and reluctant.

"Was there any evidence that someone had broken into the museum or had been locked up in the place all night?"

"None."

Qwilleran was warming up. "In other words, it could have been an inside job. How was it removed from the case? Was the case broken?"

"No. The vitrine had been properly removed and replaced."

"What's a vitrine?"

"The glass dome that protects the objects on a pedestal."

"There were other objects under the same dome, were there?"

"Yes."

"But they were not touched."

"That's right."

"How do you remove one of those domes? I looked at them, and I couldn't figure it out."

"It fits down over the pedestal, secured by a molding attached with concealed screws."

"In other words," said Qwilleran, "you'd have to know the trick in order to get the thing apart. The dagger must have been taken by somebody in the know—after hours, when the museum was closed. Wouldn't you say it looks like an inside job?"

"I dislike your reference to an *inside job*, Mr. Qwilleran," said the curator. "You newspapermen can be extremely obnoxious, as this museum has discovered—to its sorrow. I forbid you to print anything about this incident without permission from Mr. Farhar."

"You don't tell a newspaper what to print and what not to print," said Qwilleran, keeping his temper in check.

"If this item appears," Smith said, "we will have to conclude that the *Daily Fluxion* is an irresponsible, sensational press. First, you may be spreading a false alarm. Second, you may encourage an epidemic of thefts. Third, you may impede the recovery of the dagger if it has actually been stolen."

"I'll leave that up to my editor," said Qwilleran. "By the way, do you move up the ladder when Farhar leaves?"

"His successor has not yet been announced," Smith said, and his sallow skin turned the color of parchment.

Qwilleran went to dinner at the Artist and Model, a snug cellar hideaway favored by the culture crowd. The background music was classical, the menu was French, and the walls were hung with works of art. They were totally unviewable in the cultivated gloom of the basement, and even the food—small portions served on brown earthenware—was difficult for the fork to find.

It was an atmosphere for conversation and handholding, rather than eating, and Qwilleran allowed himself a moment of self-pity when he realized he was the only one dining alone. He thought, Better to be at home sharing a slice of meat loaf with Koko and having a fast game of Sparrow. Then he remembered dolefully that Koko had deserted him.

He ordered *ragôut de boeuf Bordelaise* and entertained himself by brooding over the golden dagger. The Smith person had been furtive. He had admittedly lied at the beginning of the interview. Even the girl in the checkroom had tried to deter Qwilleran from visiting the Florentine Room. Who was covering up for whom?

If the dagger had been stolen, why had the thief selected this particular memento of Renaissance Italy? Why steal a weapon? Why not a goblet or bowl? It was hardly the kind of trinket that a petty thief could peddle for a meal ticket, and professional jewel thieves—big operators—would have made a bigger haul. Someone had coveted that dagger, Qwilleran told himself, because it was gold, or because it was beautiful.

It was a poetic thought, and Qwilleran blamed it on the romantic mood of the restaurant. Then he let his thoughts drift pleasantly to Zoe. He wondered how long it would be before he could conventionally invite her out to dinner. A widow who didn't believe in funerals and who wore purple silk trousers as mourning attire apparently did not cling to convention.

All around him couples were chattering and laughing. Repeatedly one female voice rose in a trill of laughter. There was no doubt about that voice. It belonged to Sandy Halapay. She had evidently found a dinner date to amuse her while her husband was in Denmark.

When Qwilleran left the restaurant, he stole a glance at Sandy's table and at the dark head bending toward her. It was John Smith.

Qwilleran plunged his hands in his overcoat pockets and walked the few blocks to Penniman School, his mind flitting from the Cellini dagger to the sly-eyed John Smith—to the conniving Sandy—to Cal Halapay in Denmark—to Tom, the Halapay's surly houseboy—to Tom's girl in the museum checkroom—and back to the dagger.

This mental merry-go-round gave Qwilleran a mild vertigo, and he tried to shake the subject out of his mind. After all, it was none of his business. Neither was the murder of Earl Lambreth. Let the police solve it.


At Penniman School, Qwilleran found other mysteries to confound him. The Happening was a roomful of people, things, sounds and smells that seemed to have no purpose, no plan and no point.

The school was lavishly endowed (Mrs. Duxbury had been

a Penniman before her marriage), and among its facilities was an impressive sculpture studio. It had been described in one of Mountclemens' columns as "big as a barn and artistically productive as a haystack." This sculpture studio was the scene of the Happening, to attend which students paid a dollar and the general public paid three. Proceeds were earmarked for the scholarship fund.

When Qwilleran arrived, the vast room was dark except for a number of spotlights that played on the walls. These shafts and puddles of light revealed a north wall of opaque glass and a lofty ceiling spanned by exposed girders. There was also a network of temporary scaffolding overhead.

Below, on the concrete floor, persons of all ages stood in clusters or promenaded among the stacks of huge empty cartons that transformed the room into a maze. These cardboard towers, painted in gaudy colors and piled precariously high, threatened to topple at the slightest instigation.

Other threats dangled from the scaffolding. A sword hung from an invisible thread. There were bunches of green balloons, red apples tied by the stems, and yellow plastic pails filled with nobody-knew-what. A garden hose dribbled in desultory fashion. Suspended in a rope sling was a nude woman with long green hair who sprayed cheap perfume from an insecticide gun. And in the center of the scaffold, presiding over the Happening like an evil god, was "Thing #36" with its spinning eyes. Something had been added, Qwilleran noted; the Thing now wore a crown of doorknobs, Nino's symbol of death.

Soon the whines and bleeps of electronic music filled the room, and the spotlights began to move in coordination with the sound, racing dizzily across the ceiling or lingering on upturned faces.

In one passage of light Qwilleran recognized Mr. and Mrs. Franz Buchwalter, whose normal dress was not unlike the peasant costumes they had worn to the Valentine Ball. The Buchwalters immediately recognized his moustache.

"When does the Happening start?" he asked them.

"It has started," said Mrs. Buchwalter.

"You mean this is it? This is all there is?"

"Other things will Happen as the evening progresses," she said.

"What are you supposed to do?"

"You can stand around and let them Happen," she said, "or you can cause things to Happen, depending on your philosophy of life. I shall probably shove some of those cartons around; Franz will just wait until they fall on him."

"I'll just wait until they fall on me," said Franz.

As more people arrived, the crowd was being forced to circulate. Some were passionately serious; some were amused; others were masking discomfiture with bravado.

"What is your opinion of all this?" Qwilleran asked the Buchwalters, as the three of them rambled through the maze.

"We find it an interesting demonstration of creativity and development of a theme," said Mrs. Buchwalter. "The event must have form, movement, a dominant point of interest, variety, unity—all the elements of good design. If you look for these qualities, it adds to the enjoyment."

Franz nodded in agreement. "Adds to the enjoyment."

"The crew is mounting the scaffold," said his wife, "so the Happenings will accelerate now."

In the flashes of half-light provided by the moving spotlights, Qwilleran saw three figures climbing the ladder. There was the big figure of Butchy Bolton in coveralls, followed by Tom LaBlanc, and then Nino, no less unkempt than before.

"The young man with a beard," said Mrs. Buchwalter, "is a rather successful alumnus of the school, and the other is a student. Miss Bolton you probably know. She teaches here. It was her idea to have that goggle-eyed Thing reigning over the

Happening. Frankly, we were surprised, knowing how she feels about junk sculpture. Perhaps she was making a point. People worship junk today."

Qwilleran turned to Franz. "You teach here at Penniman, don't you?"

"Yes, he does," said Mrs. Buchwalter. "He teaches watercolor."

Qwilleran said, "I see you're having a show at the Westside Gallery, Mr. Buchwalter. Is it a success?"

"He's sold almost everything," said the artist's wife, "in spite of that remarkable review by George Bonifield Mountclemens. Your critic was unable to interpret the symbolism of Franz's work. When my husband paints sailboats, he is actually portraying the yearning of the soul to escape, white-winged, into a tomorrow of purest blue. Mountclemens used a clever device to conceal his lack of comprehension. We found it most amusing."

"Most amusing," said the artist.

"Then you're not offended by that kind of review?"

"No. The man has his limitations, as we all do. And we understand his problem. We are most sympathetic," said Mrs. Buchwalter.

"What problem do you mean?"

"Mountclemens is a frustrated artist. Of course, you know he wears a prosthetic hand—remarkably realistic—actually made by a sculptor in Michigan. It satisfies his vanity, but he is no longer able to paint."

"I didn't know he had been an artist," Qwilleran said. "How did he lose his hand?"

"No one seems to know. It happened before he came here. Obviously the loss has warped his personality. But we must learn to live with his eccentricities. He is here to stay. Nothing, we understand, could uproot him from that Victorian house of his—"

A series of squeals interrupted Mrs. Buchwalter. The garden hose suspended overhead had suddenly doused a number of spectators.

Qwilleran said, "The Lambreth murder was shocking news. Do you have any theories?"

"We don't allow our minds to dwell on that sort of thing," said Mrs. Buchwalter.

"We don't dwell on it," said her husband.

Now laughter filled the studio as the crew released a bale of chicken feathers and an electric fan sent them swirling like snow.

"It seems like good clean fun," Qwilleran commented.

He changed his mind a moment later when a noxious wave of hydrogen sulfide was released by the crew.

"It's all symbolic," said Mrs. Buchwalter. "You don't have to agree with the fatalistic premise, but you must admit they are thinking and expressing themselves."

Shots rang out. There were shouts, followed by a small riot among the spectators. The crew on the scaffold had punctured the green balloons, showering favors on the crowd below.

Qwilleran said, "I hope they're not planning to drop that sword of Damocles."

"Nothing really dangerous ever happens at a Happening," said Mrs. Buchwalter.

"No, nothing dangerous," said Mr. Buchwalter.

The crowd was milling about the floor, and the towers of cartons were beginning to topple. A shower of confetti descended from above. Then a volley of rubber balls, dumped from one of the yellow plastic buckets. Then—

"*Blood!*" shrieked a woman's voice. Qwilleran knew that scream, and he rammed his way through the crowd to reach her side.

Sandy Halapay's face dripped red. Her hands were red. She

stood there helplessly while John Smith tenderly dabbed at it with his handerchief. She was laughing. It was ketchup.

Qwilleran went back to the Buchwalters. "It's getting kind of wild," he said. The crowd had started throwing the rubber balls at the crewmen on the scaffold.

The rubber balls flew through the air, hit the scaffolding, bounced back, richocheted off innocent skulls, and were thrown again by jeering spectators. The music screeched and blatted. Spotlights swooped in giddy arcs.

"Get the monster!" someone yelled, and a hail of balls pelted the Thing with spinning eyes.

"No!" shouted Nino. "Stop!"

Seen in flashes of light, the Thing rocked on its perch.

"Stop!"

Crew members rushed to save it. The planks of the scaffold rattled.

"Look out!"

There was a scream from the girl in the rope sling.

The crowd scattered. The Thing fell with a crash. And with it a body plunged to the concrete floor.

# CHAPTER TWELVE

Two news items rated headlines in the Tuesday morning edition of the *Daily Fluxion*.

A valuable gold dagger, attributed to Cellini, had disappeared from the art museum. Although its absence had been noted by a guard more than a week ago, the matter was not reported to the police until a *Fluxion* reporter discovered that the rare treasure was missing from the Florentine Room. Museum officials gave no satisfactory explanation for the delay.

The other item reported a fatal accident.

"An artist plunged to death Monday night at the Penniman School of Fine Art during an audience-participation program called a Happening. He was a sculptor known professionally as Nine Oh Two Four Six Eight Five, whose real name was Joseph Hibber.

"Hibber was perched on a high scaffold in the darkened room when unruly activity on the floor below caused a near-accident to one of the mammoth props in the show.

"Eyewitnesses reported that Hibber attempted to save the object from falling on the spectators. In the effort he apparently lost his footing, falling 26 feet to a concrete floor.

"Mrs. Sadie Buchwalter, wife of Franz Buchwalter, a faculty member, was injured by a flying doorknob when the object crashed. Her condition was described as satisfactory.

"Some 300 students, faculty members and art patrons attending the benefit event witnessed the accident."

Qwilleran threw the newspaper on the bar at the Press Club that afternoon, when Arch Riker met him for a five-thirty pick-me-up.

"Plunged to his death," said Qwilleran, "or was pushed."

"You've got a criminous mind," said Arch. "Isn't one murder on your beat enough to keep you happy?"

"You don't know what I know."

"Let's have it. Who was this character?"

"A beatnik who happened to like Zoe Lambreth. And she was pretty fond of him, although you'd find this hard to believe if you could see the guy—a nature boy straight from the city dump."

"You never know about women," said Arch.

"And yet I've got to admit the boy had possibilities."

"So who pushed him?"

"Well, there's this woman sculptor, Butchy Bolton, who seemed to resent him. I think Butchy was jealous of this beatnik's friendship with Zoe and jealous of him professionally. He enjoyed more critical success than she did. Butchy also had a crush on Zoe."

"Oh, one of those!"

"Zoe was trying to brush her off—subtly—but Butchy is as subtle as a bulldog. And here's an interesting point: both Butchy and Nino, the deceased, had serious grudges against Zoe's husband. Suppose one of them killed Earl Lambreth; did Butchy consider Nino a competitor for Zoe's attention and push him off the scaffold last night? The whole crew rushed out on those flimsy boards to stop the Thing from crashing. Butchy would have had a beautiful opportunity."

"You seem to know more than the police."

"I don't have any answers. Just questions. And here's another one: Who stole the painting of a ballet dancer from Earl Lambreth's office? Last weekend I suddenly remembered it was missing on the night of the murder. I told Zoe, and she reported it to the police."

"You've been a busy boy. No wonder you haven't finished that profile on Halapay."

"And one more question: Who stole the dagger at the museum? And why are they being so cagey about it?"

"Do you have anymore yarns?" asked Arch. "Or can I go home to my wife and kiddies?"

"Go home. You're a lousy audience. Here comes a couple of guys who'll be interested."

Odd Bunsen and Lodge Kendall were walking through the bar single file.

"Hey, Jim," said Odd, "did you write that piece about the missing dagger at the museum?"

"Yeah."

"They've found it. I went up and got some shots of it. The Picture Desk thought people would like to see what the thing looked like—after all the hullabaloo you stirred up."

"Where'd they find it?"

"In the safe in the Education Department. One of the instructors was writing a piece on Florentine art for some magazine, and he took the dagger out of the case to examine. Then he went off to a convention somewhere and parked it in the safe."

"Oh," said Qwilleran. His moustache drooped.

"Well, that solves one of your problems," Arch told him. He turned to the police reporter. "Anything new in the Lambreth case?"

"A major clue just fizzled out," said Kendall. "The police

found a valuable painting that Lambreth's wife said was missing."

"Where'd they find it?" Qwilleran demanded.

"In the stock room of the gallery, filed under G."

"Oh," said Qwilleran.

Arch slapped him on the back. "As a detective, Jim, you're a great art writer. Why don't you bear down on that Halapay profile and leave crime to the police? I'm going home."

Arch left the Press Club, and Odd Bunsen and Lodge Kendall drifted away, and Qwilleran sat alone, peering unhappily into his tomato juice.

Bruno, wiping the bar, said with his wise smile, "You want another Bloody Mary without vodka, lime, Worcestershire or Tabasco?"

"No," snapped Qwilleran.

The bartender lingered. He tidied up the bar. He gave Qwilleran another paper napkin. Finally he said, "'Would you like to see a couple of my presidential portraits?"

Qwilleran glowered at him,

"I've finished Van Buren," said Bruno, "and I've got him and John Quincy Adams here under the bar."

"Not tonight. I'm not in the mood."

"I don't know anybody else who makes collage portraits out of whiskey labels," Bruno persisted.

"Look, I don't care if you make mosaic portraits out of used olive pits! I don't want to look at them tonight!"

"You're beginning to sound like Mountclemens," said Bruno.

"I've changed my mind about that drink," said Qwilleran. "I'll take one. Make it a Scotch—straight."

Bruno shrugged and began filling the order in slow motion.

"And snap it up," said Qwilleran.

Over the loudspeaker came a muffled voice that he did not hear.

"Mr. Qwilleran," said Bruno. "I think they're paging you."

Qwilleran listened, wiped his moustache, and in bad humor went to the telephone.

A soft voice said, "Mr. Qwilleran, I hope I'm not intruding, but I wonder if you have any plans for dinner tonight?"

"No, I haven't," he said, shifting gears.

"Would you come out and have dinner with me at the house? I'm feeling blue, and it would help if I could talk with someone who is understanding. I promise not to dwell on my troubles. We'll talk about pleasant things."

"I'll grab a cab and be right there."

On the way out of the Press Club, Qwilleran threw Bruno a dollar. "Drink the Scotch yourself," he said.

When Qwilleran returned home from Zoe's house sometime after midnight, he was in a congenial mood. The night was bitter cold, and yet he felt warm. He gave a quarter to a frozen-looking panhandler shuffling down Blenheim Place, and he whistled a tune as he unlocked the outer door of No. 26.

Even before he inserted the second key in the inner door, he could hear a wail from Koko in the hall.

"Ha! fair-weather friend," he said to the cat. "You snubbed me yesterday. Don't expect a game of Sparrow tonight, old fellow."

Koko was sitting on the bottom step in a tall posture. No prancing. No ankle-rubbing. He was strictly business. He spoke again urgently.

Qwilleran looked at his watch. The cat should have been asleep at this hour, curled on the refrigerator cushion in Mountclemens' apartment. But there he was, wide awake and speaking in long, loud terms. It was not the complaining whine he used when dinner was slightly delayed, nor the scolding tone he assumed when dinner was unforgivably late. It was a cry of desperation.

"Quiet, Koko! You'll wake up the house," Qwilleran said in a hushed voice.

Koko lowered his volume but persisted in the urgency of his message. He stalked back and forth on taut legs, rubbing against the newel-post.

"What's the matter, Koko? What are you trying to say?"

The cat's sleek side ground against the newel-post as if to gouge out chunks of fur. Qwilleran reached down and stroked the arched back; the silky fur had become strangely coarse and bristling. At the touch of the hand, Koko bounded up five or six stairs, then lowered his head and twisted his neck until he could rub the back of his ears against the front edge of a tread.

"Are you locked out, Koko? Let's go up and see."

Immediately the cat scampered to the top of the flight, with the man following.

"The door's open, Koko," Qwilleran whispered. "Go in. Go to sleep."

The cat squeezed through the narrow opening, and Qwilleran was halfway downstairs again when the wailing resumed. Koko had come out and was rubbing his head violently against the doorjamb.

"You can't keep that up all night! Come on home with me. I'll find you a snack." Qwilleran grabbed the cat under the middle and carried him to his own apartment, where he tossed him lightly on the sofa, but Koko was gone again in a white blur of speed, flying up the stairs and wailing desperately from the top.

At that point Qwilleran's moustache quivered without explanation. What was this all about? Without another word, he followed the cat upstairs. First he knocked on the open door. When there was no answer, he went in. The living room was dark.

As he pressed the switch, all the hidden spotlights flicked their tiny beams on paintings and objects of art. Koko was quiet now, watching Qwilleran's feet as they walked through the living room, into the dining alcove, then out again. The heavily draped and carpeted rooms had a stifling hush. When the feet stopped moving, Koko rushed off down the long hall to the dark kitchen. The feet followed. Bedroom and bathroom doors stood open. Qwilleran turned on the kitchen light.

"What is it, you devil?"

The cat was rubbing against the back door that led to the fire escape.

"If you just want to go for a walk, I'll wring your neck. Is that what you want?"

Koko rose on his hind feet and pawed at the doorknob.

"Well, I'm not taking you out. Where's your roommate? Let *him* take you out. . . . Besides, it's too cold for cats out there."

Qwilleran switched off the kitchen light and started back down the long hallway, only to have Koko come racing after him with a chesty growl. The cat threw himself at the man's legs.

Qwilleran's moustache sent him another message. He returned to the kitchen, turned on the light and took the flashlight from the broom closet. He reached for the night latch on the back door and found it unlocked. Strange, he thought.

Opening the door, he met a blast of wintry air, crackling cold. There was a wall switch just inside the door, and he flicked it with a finger, but the exterior light made only a sick puddle of yellow on the upper landing. Qwilleran thumbed the flashlight, and its powerful beam leaped about the scene below. It explored the three brick walls. It studied the closed gate. It crept over the brick paving until it pounced on the sprawled body—the long, dark, spidery body of George Boni-field Mountclemens.

Qwilleran made his way cautiously down the icy treads of the wooden staircase. He flashed the center beam of the flashlight on the side of the face. Mountclemens was lying cheek to the pavement, his body hunched. No doubt about it; he was dead.

The alley was deserted. The night was quiet. There was a fragrance of lime peel. And within the patio the only move-ment was a pale shadow just beyond the flashlight's range. It moved in circles. It was the cat, behaving oddly, performing some private ritual. With back arched and tail stiff and ears laid back, Kao K'o-Kung walked around and around and around.

Qwilleran grabbed the cat in one arm and got up the wooden staircase as fast as the icy treads would permit. At the telephone his finger hesitated over the dial, but he called the police first and after that the night city editor of the *Daily Fluxion*. Then he sat down to wait, composing his own wry versions of appropriate headlines for tomorrow's paper.

First to arrive at Blenheim Place were two officers in a patrol car.

Qwilleran told them, "You can't reach the patio from the front of the house. You have to go upstairs through his apartment and down the fire escape, or else go around the block and come in the alley gate. It may be locked."

"Who lives in the downstairs rear?" they asked.

"No one. It's used for storage."

The officers tried the door of the rear apartment and found it locked. They went upstairs and down the fire escape.

Qwilleran told them, "At first I thought he'd fallen down

the steps. They're treacherous. But he's lying too far from the bottom."

"Looks like a body wound," they said. "Looks like it might have been a knife."

Upstairs the cat arched his back and made long legs and stepped lightly in a pattern of ever-narrowing circles.

# CHAPTER THIRTEEN

The day after the murder of Mountclemens, there was only one topic of conversation at the *Daily Fluxion*. One by one they stopped at Qwilleran's desk: the members of the City Room, the Women's Department, Editorial, the Photo Lab, and the Sports Department. The head librarian, the foreman of the Composing Room, and the elevator starter paid unexpected visits.

Qwilleran's telephone rang incessantly. Women readers cried in his ear. Several anonymous callers said they were glad; Mountclemens had it coming to him. Some urged the newspaper to offer a reward for the killer. Six galleries telephoned to inquire who would review their March exhibitions, now that the critic was out of the picture. A crank called with a phony-sounding tip on the murder and was referred to the Homicide Bureau. A twelve-year-old girl applied for the job of art critic.

One call was from Sandy Halapay's maid, canceling the lunch date scheduled with Qwilleran; there was no explanation. So at noon he went to the Press Club with Arch Riker, Odd Bunsen and Lodge Kendall.

They took a table for four, and Qwilleran went over the

incident in detail, starting with Koko's unusual behavior. Mountclemens had been knifed in the stomach. The weapon had not been found. There was no sign of a tussle. The gate to the alley was locked.

"The body's being sent to Milwaukee," Qwilleran told his audience. "Mountclemens mentioned that he had a sister there, and the police found her address. They also impounded the tape reels he had been working on."

Arch said, "They've been looking at back files of his reviews, but I don't know what they hope to find. Just because he insulted half the artists in town, that doesn't make them all suspects, does it? Or maybe it does!"

"Every scrap of information helps," said Lodge.

"A lot of people hated Mountclemens. Not only artists but dealers, museum people, teachers, collectors—and at least one bartender that I know," said Qwilleran. "Even Odd wanted to bust a camera over his head."

Arch said, "The switchboard has been jumping. Everybody wants to know who did it. Sometimes I think our readers are all morons."

"Mountclemens wasn't wearing his artificial hand when he was killed," said Odd. "I wonder why."

"That reminds me," said Qwilleran. "I got quite a jolt this morning. Went upstairs to Mountclemens' apartment to get the cat's meat, and there on the top shelf of the refrigerator was that plastic hand! I jumped a foot!"

"What does the cat think about all the uproar?"

"He's edgy. I'm keeping him in my apartment, and he jumps at the slightest sound. After the police had gone last night and everything quieted down, I put a blanket on the sofa and tried to make him bed down, but he just walked the floor. I think he prowled all night."

"I'd like to know what that cat knows."

Qwilleran said, "I'd like to know what Mountclemens was

doing in the patio on a cold winter night—in his velvet house jacket. That's what he was wearing—and a glove on his good hand. Yet he had taken his topcoat with him. There was a British tweed lying on the bricks in a corner of the patio. They assume it was his—right size, New York label, and a shoulder cape! Who else would wear a cape?"

"Exactly where did you find the body?"

"In a corner of the yard, close to the gate that leads into the alley. It looked as if he'd had his back to the brick wall—the side wall, that is—when someone plunged the knife into his gut."

"It went into the abdominal aorta," said Lodge. "He didn't have a chance."

"Now we've got to find a new art critic," said Arch. "Do you want the job, Jim?"

"Who? Me? Are you crazy?"

"That gives me an idea," Lodge said. "Was there anyone in town who wanted to get Mountclemens' job for himself?"

"It doesn't pay enough to be worth the risk of a murder rap."

"But it has prestige," said Qwilleran, "and some art expert might see it as a chance to play God. A critic can make or break an artist."

"Who would be qualified for such a job?"

"A teacher. A curator. Someone who contributes to art journals."

Arch said, "He'd have to know how to write. Most artists can't write. They think they can, but they can't."

"It'll be interesting to see who applies for the job."

Someone said, "Any more dope on the Lambreth case?"

"Nothing that they've seen fit to reveal," said Lodge.

"Know who'd make a good critic?" Qwilleran said. "He's currently unemployed, too."

"Who?"

"Noel Farhar from the museum."

"Think he'd be interested?" Arch said. "Maybe I should give him a buzz."

After lunch Qwilleran spent most of the afternoon taking telephone calls, and at the end of the day his urge to go back to the Press Club for dinner was less powerful than his urge to go home and see Koko. The cat, he told himself, was now an orphan. Siamese were particularly needful of companionship. The bereaved animal had been locked up alone in Qwilleran's apartment all day. There was no telling what kind of breakdown he might have suffered.

When Qwilleran unlocked the door of his apartment, there was no sign of Koko on the sofa or the big chair, no leonine pose on the red carpet, no pale bundle of fur on the bed in the alcove.

Qwilleran called the cat's name. He got down on hands and knees and looked under things. He searched behind draperies and behind the shower curtain in the bathtub. He peered up the chimney.

He thought, I've accidentally shut him up in a cabinet or closet. But a frantic banging of doors and drawers produced no cat. He couldn't have escaped. The apartment door had been locked. There were no open windows. He's got to be in this apartment, Qwilleran thought. If I start fixing his dinner, he may come crawling out of the woodwork.

Qwilleran went to the kitchenette, approached the refrigerator, and found himself face to face with a calm, cool-eyed Koko.

Qwilleran gasped. "You devil! Were you sitting there all the time?"

Koko, huddled in an awkward pose on the refrigerator top, answered with a curt syllable.

"What's the matter, old fellow? Are you unhappy?"

The cat shifted position irritably. Now he crouched with

his body hovering above the hard porcelain surface. His haunches angled up like fins, and the fur over his shoulder blades spread open like a huge dandelion gone to seed.

"You're uncomfortable! That's what's wrong. After dinner we'll go upstairs and get your cushion. Is that okay?"

Koko squeezed both eyes.

Qwilleran started to mince the beef. "When this hunk of meat is gone, you'll have to start eating something I can afford—or else move to Milwaukee. You live better than I do."

After Koko had chewed his beef and Qwilleran had downed a salami sandwich, they went upstairs to get the blue cushion from the top of Mountclemens' refrigerator. The place was locked now, but Qwilleran still had the key the critic had given him a week ago.

Koko entered the apartment with a wondering hesitation. He wandered aimlessly, smelled the carpet here and there, and moved gradually toward one corner of the living room. The louvered doors seemed to attract him. He sniffed their edges, the hinges, the louvers—in rapt concentration.

"What are you looking for, Koko?"

The cat stretched tall on his hind legs and scratched the door. Then he pawed the red carpet.

"Do you want to get into that closet? What for?"

Koko dug vigorously at the rug, and Qwilleran took the suggestion. He opened the double doors.

In the early life of the house, this closet might have been a small sewing room or study. Now the windows were shuttered, and the space was filled with racks holding paintings in vertical slots. Some were framed; some were merely stretched canvases. Here and there Qwilleran caught glimpses of wild, meaningless splotches of color.

Once inside the closet, Koko sniffed avidly, his nose taking him to one rack after another. One particular slot interested him keenly; he tried to insert his paw.

"I'd like to know what this demonstration is all about," Qwilleran said.

Koko yowled in excitement. He tried first one paw and then the other. He took time out to brush against Qwilleran's pant leg, after which he resumed the quest.

"You want some help, I suppose. What's in that rack?" Qwilleran withdrew the framed painting that filled the narrow slot, and Koko reached in to snag a small dark object with his claws.

Qwilleran took the thing away from the cat to examine it. What could it be? Soft . . . fuzzy . . . lightweight. Koko howled in indignation.

"Sorry," said Qwilleran. "Just curious. So this is Mintie Mouse!" He tossed the mint-perfumed toy back to the cat, who clutched it with both paws, rolling on his side and pummeling it with his hind feet.

"Come on, let's get out of here." Qwilleran returned the painting to its slot but not without giving it a quick perusal. It was a dreamlike landscape filled with headless bodies and disembodied heads. He grimaced and put it away. So these were Mountclemens' blue-chip stocks!

He looked at a few more. One was a series of black lines ruled across a white background—some parallel, some intersecting. He raised his eyebrows. Another canvas was covered with gray paint—just gray paint and a signature in the lower corner. Then there was a vivid purple sphere on a red field that gave Qwilleran the beginning of a headache.

The next painting caused a peculiar sensation in the roots of his moustache. Impulsively, he swooped down on Koko, gathered him up and ran downstairs.

He went to the telephone and dialed a number that he had come to know by heart. "Zoe? This is Jim. I've found something here at the house that I want you to see. . . . A painting—one that will interest you. Koko and I went up to Mountclemens' apartment to get something, and the cat led me to this closet. He was very insistent. You'll never believe what we found. . . . A monkey. A painting of a monkey! . . . Can you come over?"

Minutes later, Zoe arrived by taxi, wearing her fur coat over slacks and a sweater. Qwilleran was watching for her. He had brought the monkey painting down to his own apartment, where it was propped on the mantel over the Monet.

"That's it!" cried Zoe. "That's the other half of Earl's Ghirotto!"

"You're sure?"

"It's obviously a Ghirotto. The brushwork is unmistakable, and the background is the same yellow-green. Notice how the design is poorly balanced; the monkey is too far to the right, and he's reaching out of the picture. Also—can't you see a scrap of the dancer's tutu showing at the right-hand edge?"

They both stared at the canvas, their thoughts taking shape.

"If this is the missing half—"

"What does it mean?"

Zoe suddenly looked hollow-cheeked. She sat down and bit her lower lip. It was the mannerism that Qwilleran had found so unpleasant in Earl Lambreth. In Zoe it was appealing.

She said, slowly, "Mountclemens knew Earl was hunting for the monkey. He was one of those who offered to buy the ballerina. And no wonder! He had found the monkey!"

Qwilleran was making short stabs at his moustache with a thumbnail. He was asking himself, Would Mountclemens kill to get the ballerina? And if that were the case, why leave the painting on the premises? Because it had been removed to the stock room and he couldn't find it? Or because—?

With a crawling sensation in his moustache, Qwilleran

remembered the gossip he had heard about Zoe and Mount-clemens.

Zoe was gazing down at her hands clasped tightly in her lap. As if she felt Qwilleran's questioning stare, she suddenly raised her eyes and said, "I despised him! I *despised* him!"

Qwilleran waited patiently and sympathetically for anything she wanted to say.

"He was an arrogant, avaricious, overbearing man," said Zoe. "I loathed Mountclemens, and yet I had to play along—for obvious reasons."

"Obvious reasons?"

"Can't you see? My paintings were enjoying his critical favor. If I had made him angry, he could have ruined my career. He would have ruined Earl, too. What could I do? I flirted—discreetly, I thought—because that was the way Mountclemens wanted to play." Zoe fussed with her handbag —clasping, unclasping, clasping. "And then he got the idea that I should leave Earl and go with him."

"How did you handle that proposition?"

"It was a delicate maneuver, believe me! I said—or I implied—that I would like to accept his proposal, but an old-fashioned sense of loyalty bound me to my husband. What an act! I felt like the heroine in one of those old silent movies."

"Did that settle the matter?"

"Unfortunately, no. He continued his campaign, and I got in deeper and deeper. It was a nightmare! There was the constant strain of acting out a lie."

"Didn't your husband know what was going on?"

Zoe sighed. "For a long time he didn't suspect. Earl was always so preoccupied with his own problems that he was blind and deaf to everyone else. But eventually he heard the gossip. And then we had a horrible scene. I convinced him— finally—that I was trapped in a nasty situation." There was prolonged business with the handbag clasp. Falteringly she said, "You know—Earl seemed to cling to me. Even though we were no longer—close—if you know what I mean. I found it *safer* to be married, and Earl clung to me because I was a success. He was born to be a failure. His only achievement was a happy accident—finding half a Ghirotto—and it was his life's ambition to find the other half and be rich!"

Qwilleran said, "You don't think Mountclemens killed your husband, do you?"

Zoe looked at him helplessly. "I don't know. I just don't know. He wouldn't have done anything so drastic merely to get me. I'm positive of that! He wasn't capable of loving that passionately. But he might have done it to get me *and* the other half of the Ghirotto."

That would be quite a package, Qwilleran reflected. He said, "Mountclemens had a passion for art."

"Only as a form of wealth, to be accumulated and hoarded. He didn't share his possessions. He didn't even want people to know he owned fabulous treasures."

"Where did he get the dough to buy them? Certainly not from writing art columns for the *Daily Fluxion*."

Zoe left his question dangling. She seemed to shrink into her chair. "I'm tired," she said. "I'd like to go home. I didn't mean to talk like this."

"I know. It's all right," Qwilleran said. "I'll call you a cab."

"Thank you for being so understanding."

"I'm complimented to have you confide in me."

Zoe bit her lip. "I feel I can say this to you: When Earl was killed, my reaction was more fear than grief—fear of Mountclemens and what would happen next. Now that fear has been removed, and I can't be anything but glad."

Qwilleran watched Zoe's taxi disappear into the darkness. He wondered if she had suspected Mountclemens from the start. Was the critic one of Earl's enemies—one of the "important people" she had been afraid to name to the police?

159

On the other hand, would a man like Mountclemens—enjoying a good life and with so much to lose—take the risk of committing murder to gain a woman and a valuable painting? Qwilleran doubted it.

Then his thoughts went back to the monkey propped on the mantel in his apartment. What would happen to it now? Along with the Rembrandt drawings and the Van Gogh, the Ghirotto monkey would go to that woman from Milwaukee. She would be unlikely to know its significance. In all probability she would loathe the ugly thing. How easy it would be—

An idea began to take shape in his mind. "Keep it . . . Say nothing . . . Give it to Zoe."

He returned to the apartment to look at the monkey. On the mantel in front of the canvas sat Kao K'o-Kung, straight as a sentinel, giving Qwilleran a reproachful stare.

"Okay. You win," said the newsman. "I'll report it to the police."

# CHAPTER FOURTEEN

Thursday morning Qwilleran telephoned Lodge Kendall at the pressroom in police headquarters.

He said, "I've picked up some information on Lambreth and Mountclemens. Why don't you bring the Homicide guys to lunch at the club?"

"Make it dinner. Hames and Wojcik are working nights."

"Do you think they're willing to discuss the case?"

"Oh, sure. Especially Hames. He's a relaxed type. Never underestimate him, though. He's got a mind like a computer."

Qwilleran said, "I'll get to the club early and snag a quiet table upstairs. Is six o'clock okay?"

"Make it six-fifteen. I won't promise, but I'll try to have them there."

Qwilleran wrote six-fifteen on his desk calendar and reluctantly considered the possibility of starting his day's work. He sharpened a handful of pencils, cleaned out his paper clip tray, filled his glue pot, straightened his stack of copy paper. Then he pulled out his draft of the Butchy Bolton interview and put it away again. No hurry; the Photo Department had not yet produced any pictures to accompany the story. Without much effort he found similar excuses to postpone most of the other chores in his "next" file.

He was in no mood to work. He was too busy wondering how the *Daily Fluxion* would react to the idea of a murderer on the staff—on the culture beat, no less! He could visualize the editorial embarrassment if the police pinned Lambreth's murder on Mountclemens, and he could picture the other newspaper gleefully capitalizing on the scandalous news. . . . No, it was unthinkable. Newspaper writers reported on homicide; they never indulged in it.

Qwilleran had liked Mountclemens. The man was a delightful host, clever writer, unashamed egotist, cat-worshipper, fearless critic, miser with electric light bulbs, sentimentalist about old houses, and an unpredictable human being. He could be curt one minute, genial the next—as he was on the night he heard the news of Lambreth's murder.

The newsman looked at his calendar. There was nothing on his schedule until six-fifteen. Six-fifteen—the hour the clock stopped for Earl Lambreth. Six-fifteen? Qwilleran felt a prickling sensation in his moustache. *Six-fifteen!* Then Mountclemens had an alibi!

It was six-twenty that evening when the police reporter turned up with the two men from the Homicide Bureau: Hames, blandly amiable, and Wojcik, all business.

Hames said, "Aren't you the fellow with the cat that can read?"

"He can not only read," said Qwilleran; "he can read backwards, and don't laugh. I'm sending him to the FBI Academy when he grows up, and he may get your job."

"He'll do all right, too. Cats are born snoopers. Our kids have a cat that gets into everything. He'd make a good cop—or a good newspaperman." Hames scanned the menu.

"Before I order, who's paying for this meal? The *Daily Fluxion* or us underpaid guardians of the public welfare?"

Wojcik said to Qwilleran, "Kendall tells us you want to talk about the art murders."

"I've picked up a few facts. Do you want to hear them now, or do you want to order first?"

"Let's hear."

"Well, it's like this: Lambreth's widow seems to have made me her confidant, and she told me a few things last night after I discovered something unusual in Mountclemens' apartment."

"What were you doing up there?"

"Looking for the cat's toy mouse. It's an old sock filled with dried mint. He was going crazy because he couldn't find it."

Hames said, "Our cat's wild for catnip, too."

"This isn't catnip. It's fresh mint that Mountclemens grew in a pot on the windowsill."

"Same thing," said Hames. "Catnip's a member of the mint family."

"So what did you find that was unusual?" said Wojcik.

"A painting of a monkey that seemed to ring a bell. I called Mrs. Lambreth, and she came over and identified it."

"What's with this monkey?"

"It has to do with that painting of a ballet dancer by Ghirotto at the Lambreth Gallery."

Hames said, "We have one of those Ghirotto dancers at home. My wife bought it for $14.95 at Sears."

"Ghirotto painted a lot of dancers," said Qwilleran, "and the reproductions are quite popular. But this one is unique. It's only half a painting. The canvas was ripped and the two halves sold separately. Lambreth owned the half with Ghirotto's signature and was hunting for the other half, which had a monkey on it. Combined and restored, they'd be worth $150,000."

Hames said, "They get ridiculous prices for art these days.
. . . Does anybody want one of these poppy-seed rolls?"

Wojcik said, "And you found the missing half—"

"In a closet in Mountclemens' apartment," said Qwilleran.

"In a closet? You were really snooping, weren't you?"

Qwilleran's moustache rebelled and he smoothed it. "I was
looking for the cat's—"

"Okay, okay. So it looks like Mountclemens killed a man to
get a picture of a dame in a short skirt. What else do you
know?"

Qwilleran, irritated by Wojcik's brusqueness, found his
spirit of cooperation flagging. He said to himself, Let him dig
up his own lousy clues. With a degree of reluctance he told
the detective, "Mountclemens had apparently been making
eyes at Mrs. Lambreth."

"Did she tell you that?"

Qwilleran nodded.

"Women always say that. Was she interested in Mountclemens?"

Qwilleran shook his head.

"Foiled!" said the jovial Hames. "So the villain went home
and committed hara-kiri in his backyard, after which he
swallowed the knife to conceal the evidence of suicide and
throw suspicion on the poor widow. Will someone please pass
the butter?"

Wojcik threw his partner an impatient scowl.

"However," said Qwilleran coolly, "I have an alibi for
Mountclemens." He paused and waited for the reaction.

Kendall was all eyes and ears; Wojcik was twiddling a
spoon; Hames was buttering another roll.

Qwilleran proceeded. "Lambreth was murdered at six-
fifteen, according to the electric desk clock that stopped at
that hour, but Mountclemens was on the three o'clock plane
to New York. I bought his ticket for him."

"You bought his ticket," said Hames, "but do you know whether he used it? Perhaps he changed his reservation and went on the seven o'clock plane after killing Lambreth at six-fifteen. . . . Funny thing about that clock stopping at six-fifteen. It wasn't damaged. It was merely unplugged from the wall socket. It appears that the murderer went to some pains to stage signs of a violent shindy, place the clock on the floor and disconnect the juice, thus pinpointing the hour of the crime. Had the struggle been genuine and had the clock been knocked to the floor accidentally in the heat of battle, it would probably have been damaged, and if it had *not* been damaged, it would have continued to run, *unless* its fall had yanked the plug from the wall socket. However, considering the position of the desk and the location of the wall socket and the spot where the clock was found, it is doubtful whether such a fall could have disconnected the plug *accidentally*. So it appears that the murderer made a special effort to register the hour of the murder by means of the clock—for the purpose of establishing an alibi—after which he took a later flight . . . all of this assuming that your art critic with a three o'clock plane ticket was actually the killer."

Wojcik said, "We'll check the airline."

After the detectives had left, Qwilleran had another cup of coffee with Lodge Kendall and said, "Did you say Hames had a mind like a computer? It's more like a cement mixer."

Kendall said, "I think he's right. I'll bet Mountclemens had you pick up his plane ticket for the express purpose of emphasizing that three o'clock departure. Then he took a later flight. Lambreth would have no qualms about letting him in the gallery after hours, and Mountclemens probably took the man completely by surprise."

"With only one hand?"

"He was tall. He came up behind Lambreth, got a strangle-hold with his right arm, and plunged the chisel in Lambreth's exposed throat with his good left hand. Then he roughed up the office, disconnected the clock, damaged some art to leave a false clue, and took a later plane."

Qwilleran shook his head. "I can't picture Mountclemens on the other end of that chisel."

"Got a better theory?"

"I'm playing with one. It hasn't jelled yet. But it might explain all three deaths. . . . What's in that package?"

"The tapes the police impounded. There's nothing on them—just an art review. Are they any good to you?"

"I'll give them to Arch," Qwilleran said. "And maybe I'll write some kind of memorial piece to go with Mountclemens' last column."

"Careful how you phrase it. You might be writing a memorial to a murderer," Kendall said.

Qwilleran's moustache made a stubborn stand. He said, "I have a hunch you'll find Mountclemens was on that three o'clock plane."

When Qwilleran arrived home with the tape reels under his arm, it was nearing eight o'clock, and Koko met him at the door with an impatient clamor. Koko was not in favor of Qwilleran's casual meal schedule.

"If you'd learn to talk, I wouldn't have to hang around the Press Club so much," the newsman explained, "and you'd get your dinner on time."

Koko passed one paw over his right ear and gave his left shoulder blade two short licks with his tongue.

Qwilleran studied the signals thoughtfully. "I guess you can talk, all right. I'm just not bright enough to read you."

After dinner, cat and man went upstairs to the dictating machine on the critic's desk, and Qwilleran slipped a reel on the spindle. The sharp voice of the late George Bonifield Mountclemens—made more nasal by the quality of the equipment—filled the room:

"For publication Sunday, March 8—Serious collectors of contemporary art are secretly acquiring all available works by the celebrated Italian painter Scrano, it was learned this week. For reasons of ill health, the artist—for twenty years a recluse in the Umbrian Hills—is no longer able to produce the paintings that have earned him the accolade of modern master.

"Scrano's final works are now en route to the United States, according to his New York agent, and prices may be expected to soar. In my own modest collection I have a small Scrano painted in 1958, and I have been offered twenty times its original cost. Needless to say, I would not part with it."

There was a pause in the dictation, while a few inches of tape unwound thoughtfully. Then the ringing voice dropped to a more casual tone.

"Correction! Editor, delete the last two sentences."

There was another pause. Then:

"Scrano's work is handled locally by the Lambreth Gallery, which will reopen soon, it has been announced. The gallery closed following the tragedy of February 25, and the art world mourns . . . correction, the *local* art world mourns . . . the passing of a respected and influential figure.

"The quality of Scrano's work has not wavered, despite age and illness. He combines the technique of an old master, the hubris of youth, the insight of a sage, the expressiveness . . ."

Koko sat on the desk, regarding the spinning tape with fascination and purring a rich throaty accompaniment.

"Recognize your old roommate?" asked Qwilleran with a note of sadness. He himself was affected by the sound of Mountclemens' last words, and he smoothed his moustache pensively.

As the tape reel rewound at high speed, Koko lowered his head and fervently rubbed his jaw against the edge of the machine.

Qwilleran said, "Who killed him, Koko? You're supposed to be able to sense things."

The cat sat tall on the desk, with forelegs close to his body, and stared at Qwilleran with wide eyes. The blue disappeared, and they were large black voids. He swayed slightly.

"Go ahead. Talk! You must know who killed him."

Koko closed his eyes and uttered a tentative squeak.

"You must have seen it happen! Tuesday night. Out the back window. Cats can see in the dark, can't they?"

The cat's ears waggled, one forward and one back, and he jumped to the floor. Qwilleran watched while he prowled about the room—aimlessly at first—looking under a chair here and a cabinet there, peering into the cold black fireplace, touching an electric cord with a wary paw. Then he thrust his head forward and down. He began to zigzag down the long hall to the kitchen, and Qwilleran followed.

At the bedroom door Koko gave a perfunctory sniff. At the threshold of the kitchen, he stopped and murmured something in his throat. Then he backtracked down the long hall to the tapestry that covered much of the wall space opposite the bedroom door. Woven into the tapestry was the scene of a royal hunting party, with horses, falcons, dogs and small game. Dim light and the fading of age made the figures almost indistinguishable, but Koko showed pronounced interest in the rabbits and wildfowl that filled one corner of the design. Was it true, Qwilleran wondered, that cats could sense the content of a picture?

Koko touched it experimentally with his paw. He reared on his hind legs and waved his head from side to side like a cobra. Then dropping to all fours, he sniffed the lower edge of the tapestry where it grazed the floor.

Qwilleran said, "Is there something behind that thing?" He lifted one corner of the heavy hanging and saw nothing but plain wall. Yet Koko gave a joyous cry. Qwilleran raised the

168

corner higher, and the cat pushed his way behind the tapestry, proclaiming his delight in positive tones.

"Wait a minute." Qwilleran went for the flashlight and shone a wedge of light between tapestry and wall. It revealed the edge of a doorframe, and that was where Koko was rubbing and sniffing and voicing his excitement.

Qwilleran followed, burrowing with some difficulty between the heavy textile and the wall, until he came to the bolted door. The catch slid open easily, and the door swung out over a narrow stairway. It made a sharp turn and descended to the floor below, where it was closed off by a second door. At one time this would have been the servants' stairs.

There was a light switch, but no light bulb responded. Qwilleran was not surprised. He descended with the aid of the flashlight—thoughtfully. If this led to the rear apartment —which the critic had claimed to use for storage—there was no telling what treasures might be found.

Koko had already scampered to the bottom and was waiting impatiently. Qwilleran picked him up and opened the door.

He found himself in a large old-fashioned kitchen with drawn window shades and the aroma of disuse. Yet the room was comfortably warm. It was more studio than kitchen. There was an easel, a table, a chair and—against one wall—a cot. Many unframed canvases stood on the floor, face to the wall.

One door led to the patio. Another, toward the front of the house, opened into a dining room. Qwilleran ran the flashlight over a marble fireplace and an ornate built-in sideboard. Otherwise the room was bare.

Koko wriggled to get free, but there was dust everywhere, and Qwilleran kept a tight hold on the cat while he turned his attention back to the kitchen.

One painting stood on the sink counter, propped against the cupboards above. It was a portrait of a steely-blue robot against a rusty-red background, disturbingly real and signed by the artist, O. Narx. There was a three-dimensional quality in the work, and the robot itself had the glint and texture of actual metal. It was covered with dust. Qwilleran had heard it said that old houses manufacture their own dust.

Alongside the back door a kitchen table, well-crusted with dried paint of many colors, held a jar of brushes, a palette knife and some twisted tubes. The easel stood near the window, and on it was another square-headed mechanical man in a menacing pose. The painting was unfinished, and a brushful of white paint splashed across the canvas had disfigured it.

Koko squirmed and squealed and made himself a troublesome armful, and Qwilleran said, "Let's get upstairs. There's nothing down here but dirt."

At the top, after bolting the door and groping his way out from under the tapestry, Qwilleran said, "False alarm, Koko. You're losing your knack. There were no clues down there."

Kao K'o-Kung gave him a withering look, then turned his back and licked himself extensively.

# CHAPTER FIFTEEN

Friday morning Qwilleran sat at his typewriter and stared at the row of keys that spelled q-w-e-r-t-y-u-i-o-p. He hated that word *qwertyuiop*; it meant that he was stymied, that he should be writing brilliant copy, and that he hadn't an idea in his head.

It was three days since he had found the body of Mountclemens sprawled in the patio. It was four days since Nino had fallen to his death. It was nine days since the murder of Earl Lambreth.

Qwilleran's moustache was twitching and sending him signals. It kept suggesting that the three deaths were connected. One person had killed the art dealer, pushed Nino off the scaffolding, and knifed Mountclemens. And yet—to spoil his argument—there was the possibility that Mountclemens had committed the first murder.

The telephone on his desk rang three times before it won his attention.

Lodge Kendall was on the line, saying, "Thought you'd like to know what Homicide found out at the airline."

"Huh? Oh, yes. What did they find out?"

"The alibi holds. The passenger list indicates Mount-clemens was on that afternoon flight."

"Did it depart on time?"

"Right on schedule. Did you know the airline puts passenger lists on microfilm and keeps them for three years?"

"No. I mean—yes. That is—thanks for filling me in."

So Mountclemens had an alibi, and Qwilleran had some support for his new theory. Only one person, he told himself, had a motive in all three crimes and the strength to plunge a blade into a man and the opportunity to push Nino to his death. Only Butchy Bolton. And yet it was all too neat, too pat. Qwilleran was reluctant to trust his suspicions.

He went back to his typewriter. He looked at the blank sheet of paper waiting expectantly. He looked at the ten green typewriter keys: qwertyuiop.

Butchy, he was aware, had a serious grudge against Earl Lambreth. She thought he had cheated her out of a lucrative commission and considerable prestige. Furthermore, Lambreth was encouraging his wife to drop Butchy. Grievances like these could build up in the imagination of a woman who had a personality problem and was given to violent fits of temper. With Lambreth out of the way, she might reason, Zoe would again be her "best friend" as in the old days. But there was another obstacle in Butchy's way: Zoe was showing inordinate interest in Nino. If Nino were to meet with a fatal accident, Zoe might have more time and enthusiasm for her girlhood friend.

Qwilleran whistled through his moustache as he remembered another fact: It had been Butchy's idea, according to Mrs. Buchwalter, to put that piece of junk sculpture on the scaffolding.

After Nino's death Butchy faced other complications. Mountclemens was posing a threat to Zoe's happiness and her career, and Butchy—fiercely protective—might see a chance to eliminate this distressing dilemma. . . . qwertyuiop.

"Do you always look so puzzled when you write?" asked a soft voice.

Startled, Qwilleran could only splutter. He jumped to his feet.

Zoe said, "I'm sorry. I shouldn't have come to your office without telephoning first, but I was downtown having my hair done, and I took a chance on finding you here. The girl at the desk said I could walk right in. Am I interrupting something important?"

"Not at all," Qwilleran said. "Glad you dropped in. Let's go to lunch."

Zoe was looking strikingly handsome. He pictured himself ushering her into the Press Club, basking in curious stares, answering questions later.

But Zoe said, "Not today, thanks. I have another appointment. I'd just like to talk to you for a few minutes."

Qwilleran found a chair for her, and she pulled it close to his.

In a low voice she said, "There's something I should tell you—something that's been on my conscience—but it isn't easy to discuss."

"Will it help the investigation?"

"I don't know, really." She glanced around the room. "Is it all right to talk here?"

"Perfectly safe," Qwilleran said. "The music critic has his hearing aid turned off, and the man at the next desk has been in a fog for two weeks. He's writing a series on income tax."

Zoe smiled meagerly and said, "You asked me how Mount-clemens could afford to buy his art treasures, and I evaded the question. But I've decided that you should be told, because indirectly it reflects on this newspaper."

"In what way?"

173

"Mountclemens was taking the profits from the Lambreth Gallery."

"You mean your husband paid him off?"

"No. Mountclemens owned the Lambreth Gallery."

"He *owned* it?"

Zoe nodded. "Earl was only an employee."

Qwilleran puffed through his moustache. "What a setup! Mountclemens could write free plugs for his own merchandise and blast the competition—and the *Flux* paid him to do it! Why didn't you tell me this before?"

Zoe's hands fluttered. "I was ashamed of Earl's connection in the deal. I guess I hoped the secret would die with him."

"Did your husband discuss gallery business at home?"

"Not until recently. I had no idea of Mountclemens' connection with the gallery until a few weeks ago. When Earl and I had the showdown over Mountclemens. It was then he told me what kind of operator Mountclemens really was. It came as a complete shock."

"That I can believe."

"I was even more appalled at Earl's involvement. After that he began to tell me more about the gallery operation. He had been under a terrible strain, and he was overworked. Well paid, but overworked. Mountclemens wouldn't hire any help —or didn't dare. Earl did everything. Besides meeting the public and coping with artists, he made the picture frames and kept the books. My husband used to work for an accounting firm."

"Yes, I'd heard that," said Qwilleran.

"Earl had to take care of all the government red tape and juggle the figures on the tax returns."

"Juggle them, did you say?"

Zoe smiled bitterly. "You don't suppose a man like Mountclemens reported all his income, do you?"

"What did your husband think about that bit of snookery?"

"He said it was Mountclemens' funeral—not his. Earl merely did what he was told, and he wasn't liable." Zoe bit her lip. "But my husband kept a complete record of actual sales."

"You mean he kept two sets of books?"

"Yes. For his own information."

Qwilleran said, "Was he intending to use that information—?"

"Earl was getting to the end of his rope. Something had to be done—some change in the arrangement. And then there was this—this unpleasantness about me. That's when Earl confronted Mountclemens with some demands."

"Did you hear their discussion?"

"No, but Earl told me about it. He threatened Mountclemens—if he didn't leave me alone."

Qwilleran said, "I don't imagine our late art critic would scare very easily."

"Oh, yes, he was scared," said Zoe. "He knew my husband wasn't joking. Earl threatened to tip off the Internal Revenue people. He had the records that would prove fraud. He would even get a commission from the government for informing."

Qwilleran leaned back in his chair. "Wow!" he said softly. "That would have blown the whole mess wide open."

"The ownership of the gallery would have been exposed, and I'm afraid the *Daily Fluxion* would have looked rather bad."

"That's putting it mildly! The other newspaper would really make hay out of a thing like that. And Mountclemens—"

"Mountclemens would have to stand trial, Earl said. It would mean a jail term for fraud."

175

"It would have been the end of Mountclemens—here or anywhere else."

They stared at each other in silence, and then Qwilleran said, "He was a complex character."

"Yes," Zoe murmured.

"Did he really know art?"

"He had a brilliant knowledge. And in spite of his crooked streak, there was no misrepresentation in his column. Whatever he praised at the Lambreth Gallery was praiseworthy—the stripe paintings, the graphics, Nino's junk sculpture—"

"What about Scrano?"

"His concept is obscene, but the technique is flawless. His work has a classic beauty."

"All I see is a flock of triangles."

"Ah, but the proportions—the design—the depth and mystery in a flat composition of geometrics! Superb! Almost too good to be true."

Qwilleran challenged her boldly. "What about your own painting? Is it as good as Mountclemens said?"

"No. But it will be. The dirty colors I used expressed my inner turmoil, and that's all over now." Zoe showed Qwilleran a cold-blooded little smile. "I don't know who killed Mountclemens, but it's the best thing that could have happened." Venom darted from her eyes. "I don't think there's any doubt that he killed my husband. That night when Earl had to stay in his office to work on the books . . . I think he was expecting Mountclemens."

"But the police say Mountclemens left for New York at three o'clock that afternoon—by plane."

"I don't think so. I think he drove to New York—in that station wagon that was parked in the alley." Zoe stood up to leave. "But they'll never prove anything now that he's gone."

As Qwilleran rose, she extended a hand in a soft leather glove. She did it almost with gaiety. "I must hurry. I have an appointment at Penniman School. They're taking me on the faculty." Zoe smiled radiantly and walked from the office with a light step.

Qwilleran watched her go and said to himself, She's free now, and she's happy. . . . Who freed her? Then he hated himself for his next thought. And if it was Butchy, I wonder if the plot was entirely Butchy's idea.

For a while Professional Suspicion argued with Personal Inclination.

The latter said, *"Zoe is a lovely woman, incapable of such a heinous plot. And she sure knows how to wear clothes!"*

To which Professional Suspicion replied, "She's pretty eager to have her husband's murder blamed on the critic, now that he's gone and can't defend himself. She keeps coming up with scraps of information—strictly afterthoughts—that make Mountclemens look like a heel."

*"But she's so gentle and appealing and talented and intelligent! And that voice! Like velvet."*

"She's a smart dame, all right. Two people stabbed . . . and she gets the jackpot. It would be interesting to know how those maneuvers were engineered. Butchy may have done the dirty work, but she isn't bright enough to hatch the plot. Who gave her the key to the back door of the gallery? And who told Butchy to vandalize the female figure—in order to throw suspicion on a cockeyed male? Zoe wasn't even interested in Butchy; she was just using her."

*"Yes, but Zoe's eyes! So deep and honest."*

"You can't trust a woman with eyes like that. Just stop and think what probably happened on the night of Mountclemens' murder. Zoe phoned him to arrange a rendezvous, saying she'd drive into the deserted alley and sneak in the back way. That's probably the way she always did it. She'd blow the horn, and Mountclemens would go out and unlock the patio gate. But the last time it happened, it wasn't Zoe standing there in the dark; it was Butchy—with a short, wide, sharp, pointed blade."

"*But Zoe is such a lovely woman. And that gentle voice! And those knees!*"

"Qwilleran, you're a dope. Don't you remember how she got you out of the way on the night of Mountclemens' murder by inviting you to dinner?"

That evening Qwilleran went home and sat down and said to Qwilleran, "You fell for that helpless-female act and let her make you a stooge. . . . Remember how she sighed and bit her lip and stammered and called you so *understanding?* All the time she was building up her case with hints, alibis, painful revelations. . . . And did you notice that nasty gleam in her eye today? It was the same savage look she put in that cat picture at the Lambreth Gallery. Artists always paint themselves. You've found that out."

Qwilleran was plunged in the depths of his big armchair, pulling on a pipe that had burned out some minutes before. His silence weighted the atmosphere, and a shrill protest eventually came from Koko.

"Sorry, old fellow," said Qwilleran. "I'm not very sociable tonight."

Then he sat up straight and asked himself, What about that station wagon? Did Mountclemens drive it to New York? And whose was it?

Koko spoke again, this time from the hallway. His conversation was a melodic succession of cat sounds that had a certain allure. Qwilleran walked out to the hall and found Koko frolicking on the staircase. The cat's slender legs and tiny feet, looking like long-stemmed musical notes, were playing tunes up and down the red-carpeted stairs. When he saw Qwilleran, he raced to the top of the flight and looked down with an engaging follow-me invitation in his stance and the tilt of his ears.

Qwilleran suddenly felt indulgent toward this friendly little creature who knew when companionship was needed. Koko could be more entertaining than a floor show and, at times, better than a tranquilizer. He gave much and demanded little.

Qwilleran said, "Want to visit your old stamping ground?" He followed Koko and unlocked the critic's door with the key he carried.

Trilling with delight, the cat walked in and explored the apartment, savoring every corner.

"Have a good smell, Koko. That woman from Milwaukee will be coming soon, and she'll sell the place and take you home with her, and then you'll have to live on beer and pretzels."

Koko—as if he understood and wished to comment—paused in his tour and sat down on his spine for a brief but significant washup of his nether parts.

"I gather you'd rather live with me."

The cat ambled toward the kitchen, sprang to his old post on the refrigerator, found it cushionless, complained and jumped down again. Hopefully he reconnoitered the corner where his dinner plate and water bowl used to be. Nothing there. He hopped lightly to the stove, where the burners tantalized him with whiffs of last week's boiled-over broth. From there he stepped daintily to the butcher's block, redolent with memories of roasts and cutlets and poultry. Then he nuzzled the knife rack and dislodged one blade from the magnetic bar.

"Careful!" said Qwilleran. "You could cut off a toe." He put the knife back on the magnet.

As he lined it up with the other three blades, his moustache flagged him, and Qwilleran had a sudden urge to go down to the patio.

He went to the broom closet for the flashlight and wondered why Mountclemens had gone down the fire escape

179

without it. The steps were dangerous, with narrow treads partly iced.

Had the critic thought he was going down to meet Zoe? Had he thrown his tweed coat over his shoulders and gone down *without* a flashlight? Had he taken a knife instead? The fifth knife that belonged on the magnetic rack?

Mountclemens had left his prosthetic hand upstairs. A man so vain would have worn it to meet his paramour, but he wouldn't need it to kill her.

Qwilleran turned up the collar of his corduroy jacket and stepped carefully down the fire escape, accompanied by a curious but unenthusiastic cat. The night was cold. The alley kept its after-hours silence.

The newsman wanted to see how the patio gate opened, in what direction the shadows fell, how visible an arriving visitor would be in the darkness. He examined the solid plank gate with its heavy Spanish lock and strap hinges. Mountclemens would have remained partly hidden behind the gate as he opened it. One swift movement by the visitor would have pinned him to the wall. Somehow Mountclemens had failed to take his intended victim by surprise. Somehow the murderer had managed to get the jump on him.

While Qwilleran mused and ran the flashlight over the weathered bricks of the patio, Koko discovered a dark stain on the brick floor and sniffed it intently.

Qwilleran grabbed him roughly about the middle. "Koko! Don't be disgusting!"

He went back up the fire escape, carrying the cat, who writhed and squalled as if he were being tortured.

In Mountclemens' kitchen Koko sat down in the middle of the floor and had a pedicure. His brief walk in the unclean outdoors had soiled his toes, his claws, the pads of his dainty feet. Spreading the brown toes like petals of a flower, he darted his pink tongue in and out—washing, brushing, combing and deodorizing with one efficient implement.

Suddenly the cat paused in the middle of a lick, his tongue extended and his toes spread in midair. A faint rumble came from his throat, and he unfolded to standing position—tense with subdued excitement. Then deliberately he walked to the tapestry in the long hall and pawed the corner.

"There's nothing down in that old kitchen except dust," said Qwilleran, and then his moustache tingled, and he had a singular feeling that the cat knew more than he himself did.

He picked up the flashlight, rolled up the corner of the tapestry, unbolted the door and went down the narrow service stairs. Koko was waiting at the bottom, making no sound, but when Qwilleran picked him up, he felt the cat's body vibrating, and he felt tension in every muscle.

Qwilleran opened the door and let it swing into the old kitchen, quickly flashing his light around the entire room. There was nothing there to warrant Koko's restlessness. Qwilleran trained the flashlight on the easel, the littered table, the canvases stacked against the walls.

And then with a disturbing sensation on his upper lip he realized there were fewer canvases than he had seen the night before. The easel was empty. And the robot propped on the sink was gone.

Momentarily off his guard, he lost his hold on Koko, and the cat jumped to the floor. Qwilleran swung around and flashed the light into the dining room. It was empty, as before.

In the kitchen Koko was stalking something—with stealth in every line of his body. He jumped first to the sink, teetered on the edge while he scanned the area, then noiselessly down to a chair, then up to the table. As he ran his nose over the clutter on the tabletop, his mouth opened, his whiskers flared, and he showed his teeth, while with one paw he scraped the table around the palette knife.

Qwilleran stood in the middle of the room and tried to assemble his thoughts. Something was happening here that made no sense. Who had been in this kitchen? Who had removed the paintings—and why? The two pictures of robots had disappeared. What else had been taken?

Qwilleran placed the flashlight on a tiled counter, so that the light fell on the few remaining canvases in the room, and he turned one around.

It was a Scrano! A blaze of orange and yellow triangles, the canvas was painted in the Italian artist's smooth, slick style, and yet it had a feeling of depth that made Qwilleran reach out to touch the surface. Down in the corner was the famous signature, daubed in block letters.

Qwilleran set it aside and turned another painting around to face the room. Again, triangles! These were green on blue. Behind this canvas there were more—gray on brown, brown on black, white on cream. Proportions and arrangements varied, but the triangles were all pure Scrano.

A throaty murmur from Koko attracted Qwilleran's attention. The cat was sniffing the orange triangles on the yellow background. Qwilleran wondered what it was worth. Ten thousand? Twenty thousand? Perhaps even more, now that Scrano would paint no more.

Had Mountclemens been cornering the market? Or were these forgeries? And in either case . . . who was stealing them?

Koko's nose covered the surface of the painting in great detail, as if he were experiencing the texture of the canvas, visible under the pigment. When he came to the signature, his neck was stretched, and he tilted his head first to one side and then to the other, as he strained to get close to the letters.

His nose moved from right to left, first tracing the O, then studying the N, moving on to the A, sniffing the R with gusto as if it were something special, then on to the C, and finally lingering over the S.

"Remarkable!" said Qwilleran. "Remarkable!"

He hardly heard the turning of a key in the back door, but Koko heard it. The cat vanished. Qwilleran froze, as the door slowly opened.

The figure that stood in the doorway made no move. In the half light Qwilleran saw square shoulders, heavy sweater, square jaw, high square brow.

"Narx!" said Qwilleran.

The man came to life. He sidled into the room, reaching for the table. His eyes were on Qwilleran. With a lunge he seized the palette knife and rushed forward.

Suddenly . . . shrieks . . . snarls! The room was full of flying things—swooping down, across, back, up, over!

The man ducked. The hurtling bodies were quicker than the eye. They screamed like harpies. They flew down, under, up, across. Something hit him in the arm. He faltered.

In that half moment Qwilleran pounced on the flashlight and swung it with all his force.

Narx staggered back, went down. There was a sharp, rend-ing *crack* as his head struck the tiled counter. He slumped slowly to the floor.

# CHAPTER SIXTEEN

It was five-thirty at the Press Club, and Qwilleran was relating the story for the hundredth time. All day Monday the personnel of the *Daily Fluxion* had been filing past his desk to hear the details firsthand.

At the Press Club bar Odd Bunsen said, "I wish I'd been there with my camera. I can picture our hero phoning the police with one hand and holding up his pants with the other."

"Well, I had to tie Narx with my belt," Qwilleran explained. "When his head hit the tile counter, he was out cold, but I was afraid he'd come around while I was phoning the police. I'd already tied his wrists with my necktie—my good Scotch tie—and the only thing I had for his ankles was my belt."

"How did you know it was Narx?"

"When I saw that square face and those square shoulders, I thought of those pictures of robots, and I knew this man must be the artist. Painters, I've been told, always put some quality of themselves on canvas—whether they paint kids or cats or sailboats. But Koko was the one who made it all clear when he read Scrano's signature backwards."

Arch said, "How does it feel to be playing Dr. Watson to a cat?"

Odd said, "What about the signature? That's something I missed?"

"Koko read the signature on this painting," Qwilleran explained, "and he spelled it out backwards. He always reads backwards."

"Oh, naturally. It's an old Siamese custom."

"That's when I realized that Scrano, the painter of the triangles, was also O. Narx, the painter of the robots. Their painted surfaces had the same slick metallic effect. A few minutes later the robot himself walked into the house and came at me with a palette knife. He would have got me, too, if Koko hadn't come to the rescue."

"Sounds as if that cat's in line for a Civilian Citation. What did he do?"

"He went berserk! And one Siamese flying around in a panic looks and sounds like a pack of wildcats. Zoom—screech —wham! I thought there were six animals in that room, and that fellow Narx was one bewildered guy."

"So Scrano is a fake," said Arch.

"Yep. There's no Italian recluse hiding out in the Umbrian Hills," said Qwilleran. "There's only Oscar Narx manufacturing triangle pictures for Mountclemens to plug in his column and sell in his art gallery."

"Funny why he wouldn't use his own name," said Odd.

Then Arch said, "But Mountclemens' last column said there wouldn't be anymore stuff from Scrano."

"I think Mountclemens was planning to eliminate Oscar Narx," said Qwilleran. "Maybe Narx knew too much. I suspect our critic was not on that three o'clock plane the day of Lambreth's murder. I suspect he had an accomplice who used the plane ticket and entered Mountclemens' name on the passenger list. And I'll bet that accomplice was Narx."

"And then Mountclemens took a later flight," said Arch.

"Or drove to New York," said Qwilleran, "in the mysterious station wagon that was parked behind the gallery in the late afternoon. Zoe Lambreth heard her husband talking about it on the phone."

Odd Bunsen said, "Mountclemens was crazy to let another guy in on the plot. If you're going to commit murder, go it alone, I always say."

"Mountclemens wasn't stupid," said Qwilleran. "He probably had a clever alibi figured out, but something went wrong."

Arch, who had been hearing fragments of Qwilleran's story all day, said, "What makes you so sure Mountclemens was going to kill somebody when he went down to his backyard?"

"Three reasons." Qwilleran was enjoying himself. He was speaking with authority and making large gestures. "First, Mountclemens went down to the patio to meet someone, and yet this vain man left his prosthetic hand upstairs. He wasn't going to greet a guest, so he didn't need it. Second, he did not take the flashlight, although the steps were icy and treacherous. Third, I suspect he took a kitchen knife instead; there's one missing."

Qwilleran's audience was hanging on every word.

"Apparently," he went on, "Mountclemens failed to take Narx by surprise. Unless he could surprise him and sink the knife in his back as Narx came through the gate, there was a good chance that the younger man would overpower the critic. Narx is a powerful-looking adversary, and it was one hand against two."

"How do you know Mountclemens went downstairs to meet someone?"

"He had on his lounging coat. He probably had his topcoat over his shoulders while waiting for Narx, then threw it off to get ready for action. Narx would unlock the gate, which

186

swings into the patio, and Mountclemens would be waiting behind it, ready to knife him in the back. He probably planned to deposit the body in the alley, where the murder would be blamed on a tramp. It's that kind of neighborhood."

"If Narx is as formidable as you say," said Arch, "how did that fool think he could pull off the job with one hand?"

"Vanity. Everything Mountclemens did, he did superbly. It gave him an impossible conceit. . . . And I think I know why he failed this time. It's only a guess, but here's how I figure it: When Narx was unlocking that patio gate, he was alerted to Mountclemens' presence."

"How?"

"He smelled that lime-peel scent that Mountclemens always wore."

"Cr-r-razy!" said Odd Bunsen.

Arch said, "Narx might have gotten away with murder if he hadn't come back for those paintings."

"Two murders," said Qwilleran, "if it hadn't been for Koko."

"Anybody want another drink?" Arch said. "Bruno, let's have two more martinis and a tomato juice. . . . Make it three martinis. Here comes Lodge Kendall."

"Skip the tomato juice," said Qwilleran. "I've got to leave in a couple of minutes."

Kendall was hurrying with news. "Just came from Headquarters," he said. "Narx is finally able to make a statement, and the police have his story. It's just the way Qwill said. Narx painted the Scrano pictures. Every time he came to town, he camped out in Mountclemens' vacant apartment, but mostly he worked in New York. He brought the stuff here by station wagon, posing as Scrano's New York agent."

"Did he mention the three o'clock plane flight?"

"Yes. He was the one who used Mountclemens' ticket."

Odd said, "Then Mountclemens—that hammerhead—let him in on the plot."

"No. Narx was innocent at that stage of the game. You see, he had just come to town with the wagon, and Mountclemens told him to fly right back to New York to meet a big buyer who was due in unexpectedly from Montreal. Mountclemens said he had just arranged this deal by phone—in Narx's name, the way he conducted all Scrano business. Narx understood he was to hustle back and meet the Canadian in New York at five o'clock and sell him a flock of Scrano paintings. It sounded logical enough to Narx. After all, he was front man for the operation. So Mountclemens turned his own ticket over to Narx, drove with him to the airport, and saw him off on the three o'clock plane."

"How come Mountclemens' name was on the passenger list?"

"According to Narx, they barely made it to the airport by flight time, and Mountclemens said, 'Don't bother to change the name on the ticket. Just go directly to the gate and check in.' He said he had decided to drive. He claimed he would start out immediately in Narx's station wagon, stop in Pittsburgh overnight, and arrive in New York Thursday morning."

Qwilleran said, "I can guess what went wrong."

"Well," said Kendall, "the sucker from Montreal was nuts about those triangles. He wanted all he could get. So Narx phoned Earl Lambreth and asked him to airfreight some of the older stock that hadn't sold."

"That's the phone call Zoe overheard."

"Lambreth said he'd send them by wagon, but Narx told him that Mountclemens and the station wagon were already halfway to Pittsburgh. Lambreth said no, the car was still there, parked in the alley behind the gallery."

"So Narx smelled a rat."

"Not until he heard the news of Lambreth's murder and

realized Mountclemens had lied. Then he decided to capitalize on it. He hated Mountclemens anyway; he felt like a flunkey—a robot—always carrying out the great man's orders. So he decided to hit him for a bigger cut of the dough that Mountclemens was raking in from Scrano sales."

Odd said, "Narx was dumb to think he could blackmail a sharp operator like Monty."

"So Mountclemens laid for him in the patio," said Kendall, "but Narx got the jump and grabbed the knife."

"Did he say why he returned to the scene?"

"Mostly to collect some paintings that had his own signature on them. He was afraid the police might start checking. But he also took some Scrano pictures and was going back for more when he ran into Qwill—and that cat!"

Arch said, "What will happen to the value of Scrano pictures when this story breaks? A lot of investors are going to be jumping out of high windows."

"Well, I'll tell you something," said Qwilleran. "I've looked at a lot of art in the last few weeks, and if I had some dough to squander, I think I'd buy some nice gray and white triangles by Scrano."

"Man, you're lost!" said Odd.

"I forgot to tell you," said Kendall. "Those triangle pictures were a collaboration. Narx says he painted them, but Mountclemens designed them."

"Very clever," said Qwilleran. "Mountclemens had lost a hand and couldn't paint; Narx had a great technique but no creative imagination. Pretty slick!"

"I'll bet a lot of artists have ghost-painters," said Odd.

"Come on, have another tomato juice," Arch invited. "Live it up."

"No thanks," said Qwilleran. "I'm having dinner with Zoe Lambreth, and I've got to go home and change my shirt."

"Before you go," said Odd, "maybe I should explain about that lady welder and why I didn't get any pix last week."

"No rush," said Qwilleran.

"I went to the school, but she wasn't there. She was home with a couple of sore flippers."

"What happened?"

"Remember that guy that fell and killed himself? The Bolton dame tried to save him. He fell against her hands and sprained her wrists. But she'll be back this week, and I'll get your shots."

"Make them good," Qwilleran said. "Flatter the gal, if you can."

When Qwilleran arrived home to feed the cat, he found Koko sprawled on the living room carpet taking a bath.

"Dressing for dinner?" said Qwilleran.

The pink tongue darted over white breast, brown paws and fawn flanks. Moistened pads were wiped over velvety brown ears. The lustrous brown tail was clutched between forepaws and groomed with painstaking care. Koko looked surprisingly like a cat and not the supernal creature who read minds, knew what was going to happen, smelled what he couldn't see, and sensed what he couldn't smell.

Qwilleran said, "They should have given you a headline, Koko. *Cat Sleuth Sniffs Out Double Murder Clue.* You were right every time, and I was wrong every time. Nobody stole the gold dagger. Mountclemens didn't take the three o'clock plane. Butchy didn't commit any crimes. Nino wasn't murdered. And Zoe didn't lie to me."

Koko went on licking his tail.

"But I still don't have all the answers. Why did you lead me to that closet upstairs? To get Mintie Mouse or to help me find the Ghirotto monkey?

"Why did you call attention to the knife rack Friday night?

Did you want me to know one was missing? Or were you just suggesting some chopped tenderloin?

"And why did you insist on going downstairs to that kitchen? Did you know Narx was coming?

"And how about the palette knife? Why were you trying to cover it up? Did you know what was going to happen?"

Koko went on licking his tail.

"And another thing: When Oscar Narx came at me with that blade, did you really panic? Were you just a scared cat, or were you trying to save my life?"

Koko finished his tail and gazed at Qwilleran with a faraway look, as if some divine answer was forming in his glossy brown head. Then he twisted his lithe body into a tortured shape, turned up his nose, crossed his eyes, and scratched his ear with one hind leg and an expression of catly rapture.

# A selection of bestsellers from Headline

| | | |
|---|---|---|
| APPOINTED TO DIE | Kate Charles | £4.99 ☐ |
| SIX FOOT UNDER | Katherine John | £4.99 ☐ |
| TAKEOUT DOUBLE | Susan Moody | £4.99 ☐ |
| POISON FOR THE PRINCE | Elizabeth Eyre | £4.99 ☐ |
| THE HORSE YOU CAME IN ON | Martha Grimes | £5.99 ☐ |
| DEADLY ADMIRER | Christine Green | £4.99 ☐ |
| A SUDDEN FEARFUL DEATH | Anne Perry | £5.99 ☐ |
| THE ASSASSIN IN THE GREENWOOD | P C Doherty | £4.99 ☐ |
| KATWALK | Karen Kijewski | £4.50 ☐ |
| THE ENVY OF THE STRANGER | Caroline Graham | £4.99 ☐ |
| WHERE OLD BONES LIE | Ann Granger | £4.99 ☐ |
| BONE IDLE | Staynes & Storey | £4.99 ☐ |
| MISSING PERSON | Frances Ferguson | £4.99 ☐ |

*All Headline books are available at your local bookshop or newsagent, or can be ordered direct from the publisher. Just tick the titles you want and fill in the form below. Prices and availability subject to change without notice.*

Headline Book Publishing, Cash Sales Department, Bookpoint, 39 Milton Park, Abingdon, OXON, OX14 4TD, UK. If you have a credit card you may order by telephone – 0235 400400.

Please enclose a cheque or postal order made payable to Bookpoint Ltd to the value of the cover price and allow the following for postage and packing:
UK & BFPO: £1.00 for the first book, 50p for the second book and 30p for each additional book ordered up to a maximum charge of £3.00.
OVERSEAS & EIRE: £2.00 for the first book, £1.00 for the second book and 50p for each additional book.

Name ...............................................................................................................

Address ...........................................................................................................

........................................................................................................................

........................................................................................................................

If you would prefer to pay by credit card, please complete:
Please debit my Visa/Access/Diner's Card/American Express (delete as applicable) card no:

| | | | | | | | | | | | | | | | | | |
|--|--|--|--|--|--|--|--|--|--|--|--|--|--|--|--|--|--|

Signature ......................................................... Expiry Date .........